# LIFE'S
# CHALLENGES

# LIFE'S CHALLENGES

## A SHORT STORY COLLECTION

SYLVIA BEHNISH

Order this book online at www.trafford.com
or email orders@trafford.com

Most Trafford titles are also available at major online book retailers.

Printed in the United States of America.

ISBN: 978-1-4669-3864-9(sc)
ISBN: 978-1-4669-3865-6 (e)

*Trafford rev. 05/19/2012*

 www.trafford.com

**North America & international**
toll-free: 1 888 232 4444 (USA & Canada)
phone: 250 383 6864 ♦ fax: 812 355 4082

# CONTENTS

In Memory of my parents, Max and Lilias Behnish

# HER MOTHER'S FUR COAT

PULLING THE LONG-AGO memory from the dark recesses of her brain, Martine remembered the spectre of her mother as she stood at the edge of the ditch, her fur coat dripping, and her hair thick with mud as it lay plastered against her cheeks. Her eyes, appearing like black caverns leading into her soul, sparkled brilliantly as the headlights of each passing car reflected their light.

When last Martine had turned around, she had seen her mother walking the narrow pathway between the road and the ditch dressed in her finest; a fur coat inherited from a deceased aunt, brand new rhinestone earrings and her hair newly coiffed. And because it was a rainy evening, she wore her gumboots. Anyone living on a farm knows you don't wear your best shoes when it's pouring cats and dogs, no matter what special event it is you are planning to attend.

As a young child of eight years old, to Martine this startling transformation in her mother was a shock, and one that she knew even at that tender age would stay in her memory forever, periodically bubbling up to the surface to haunt her. Before leaving home, she had admired her mother's efforts at elegance and in spite of the gumboots had thought she'd looked quite beautiful.

After getting out of the bus, Martine had walked ahead of the two women. With her head tucked into the collar of her heavy winter coat, she had slogged along, leaning into the northerly blowing wind. Struggling against the cold blast of winter she thought of the singing and dancing they would be seeing, music she knew she would love, music she'd been singing in their large kitchen for the previous two weeks.

Her only audience had been her father's canaries, budgies and finches. Each had chirped their approval at Martine's renditions and in their own unique way had caused pandemonium in the small dining area. Because her thoughts as she walked had been up on the stage with the musicians, she had failed to hear her mother's muffled calls for help. The frightened voice of her mother had been pulled into the soggy night air by the wind and rain where it was carried off to the mountains beyond.

But fortunately her mother's best friend had heard her plaintive cry for assistance. "Sir," she had called as she waved to a passing gentleman, "would you be kind enough to help my friend out of the ditch?"

As Martine remembered her mother's ditch dunk, as she now thought of it, time had not dimmed the memory of that stranger's expression as he looked first at her mother's friend, then at Martine before his eyes finally and reluctantly looked down at the sodden spectacle in the water-filled ditch.

"How did she get there?" he asked while he attempted to put off the inevitable. He appeared old in the eyes of an eight year old child but when exposed to the memory of her adult self, Martine realized he had probably been in his mid thirties, about the age she now was herself. He had no doubt been off to see the same musical event they were planning to enjoy.

With an expression of extreme sadness, he glanced down at his suit and shrugged before again looking at the sad spectacle of this strange woman helplessly ensconced in the muddy water. "Okay," he finally answered as he saw that our faces were watching him, beseeching him to help. At that moment he was our guardian angel. The only one for miles around, it appeared.

Martine, with an adult's perspective, thought that it was not the first question he should have asked. But to a young child, his question was reasonable and she had wanted to know also. She knew without a doubt that if she had ended up in the ditch wearing her very best clothes, she would've been in very big trouble and explanations would have been required to more than just this stranger.

"Thank you, Sir," Martine's mother's friend smiled. She looked ready to throw her arms around the kind man's neck in an effort to show her gratitude. He backed up to avoid the emotional onslaught, barely missing a slide down the bank into the water-filled ditch himself.

Martine remembered her efforts to suppress the giggle that had nearly escaped her. But as an adult she could now laugh out loud as she recalled the scene and the stranger's fancy footwork as he sought to regain his balance. She had admired his quickness in pulling back from the edge and had wondered briefly if he might have been one of the dancers they were going to see that evening.

Reluctantly he reached down to grab Martine's mother's muddy outstretched hand. Most people probably don't know but a fur coat that has been submerged in a water-filled ditch is not the easiest thing to pull up a bank, especially when it has a woman in it who is wearing gumboots that are filled with water.

With loud grunts on the part of the stranger, considerable groaning on the part of Martine's mother and a lot of huffing and puffing from her friend, the two of them managed to pull her to the top of the ditch. Swaying, her mother staggered slightly and grabbed again at the arm of the gentleman, attaching herself firmly to the sleeve of his suit. Steadying her, he quickly stepped back, out of range of that muddy, clutching hand. And with a nod of his head, he was gone.

"Thank you Sir," my mother called in a quavering voice to the man's quickly retreating back.

Martine remembered watching the back of the man as he anxiously brushed at his clothes. Walking quickly, he tried to put as much distance as possible between himself and the bedraggled woman he'd dredged from the ditch.

Together, in a careful row as they hugged the roadway, they slogged to where the special event was going to be held and made a bee-line for the washroom. As Martine's mother and her friend attempted to squeeze the muddy water out of the fur coat, they began to giggle. Tears actually ran down their faces in their mirth leaving streaks on Martine's mother's mud-speckled face. Martine remembered her surprise at their behavior. She couldn't believe it. 'If I had ended up in a ditch and *then* giggled, I really would've been in big, big trouble,' she had thought to herself. As an adult, she could somewhat understand their mirth but added the thought that it would only have been humorous as long as she had not been the one who had fallen into the ditch. But in spite of the giggles and guffaws, she had been sure she'd heard the chatter of her mother's false teeth.

Martine's mother used paper towels in an attempt to dry her hair but the mud refused to budge; it would be a reminder throughout the entire concert of her unplanned adventure in the ditch. They emptied the gumboots of water into the toilet bowl leaving a muddy ring around the water line. And still they giggled. Martine remembered that as she stood there watching the scene unfold before her, she realized that her normally sane mother's wet fur coat smelled like a whole roomful of wet dogs. So while they giggled, she gagged.

"Well we've got to see the show," her mother insisted. "We've come all this way and we have to wait to get the bus home anyway. And besides Martine will be so disappointed if we don't see it."

"Yes," her friend sensibly agreed. "And it will give you a chance to dry out before you have to go outside in the cold again." For some unexplainable reason, Martine remembered hearing them fall into gales of giggles again. "But we'd best avoid that ditch when we leave," her friend said with an attempt at a straight face.

With a final glance in the mirror, her hair not looking a whole lot better than when she had first been dragged from the ditch, Martine's mother led the way from the washroom, her head held high, as she made her grand entrance into the auditorium for the biggest musical of the year. Heads turned and people stared but her mother continued the march to her seat, appearing not to notice the ogling eyes and gaping mouths.

At eight years old, Martine had not yet developed any great understanding for her mother's predicament. In fact she felt extremely embarrassed to be walking down the aisle behind such a dishevelled looking woman who people might realize was her mother. Keeping her head down and tucked into the collar of her coat, Martine hoped no one from her school would recognize her.

Thinking back on the experience, Martine could now give kudos to her mother when she thought of her walking to her seat wearing squelching gumboots, her hair still in muddy wet strings, carrying a dripping fur coat that smelled like a wet dog, wearing a large smile on her 'thank God I'm out of that ditch' face but still wearing her brand new rhinestone earrings.

When asked, Martine's mother does not remember giggling—at all. She remembers very definitely that the whole episode was not a laughing matter. She said she does remember going too close to the edge of the ditch as a car flew past and sliding much too quickly into the freezing, muddy water. She also remembers feeling thankful that the ditch was not full of water and that she could touch the bottom because she couldn't imagine trying to tread water in a wet fur coat and gumboots filled with water as she tried to clutch bits of debris along its banks.

Martine realized that she finally had the answer to that stranger's long-ago question of how her mother ended up in the ditch. But, when she thought about it as an adult, that was not the most important question.

Her mother also remembered an unbelievably long evening spent sitting in very wet clothes and slimy feet but with a smile plastered onto her face like the mud in her hair looking as if there was nowhere on earth she'd rather be than at that special musical with her only daughter and her very best friend.

As mother and daughter reminisced about the good old times, Martine finally got the opportunity to ask her mother the question that had puzzled her for so many years. "Whatever happened to your lovely fur coat?"

"It was never quite the same again, my dear. At least it was no longer wearable to special events anymore even by someone as practical as I am," her mother replied with a smile. "I really felt quite uncomfortable in social circles smelling like a dog."

# THE DAY MY LIFE CHANGED

THE DAY BEGAN as each Saturday morning had for as long as I could remember. That is until I saw the box on the top shelf in my mother's closet. It wasn't seeing the box that caused the problem, but rather asking my mother about it that created the difficulties on that early weekend morning.

"Sit down, dear," she said when I raised the question about the box. Although not much bigger than a small child's shoe box and partially hidden, it was very much in evidence to a snoopy teenage girl.

Right then and there I should have declared an absolute lack of interest in it. But I didn't. Instead I smiled and waited to hear the lovely story my mother was about to tell me and to see the old pictures she'd show me. Waiting expectantly, I was convinced the box was also filled with beautiful old heirlooms that would each be fabulous stories in themselves.

"This box is full of history," she began hesitantly. "It's your history, dear." I had no problem with her words but an expression I could not read filled the hollows of her face and made her eyes dim with sadness. Based on the expression on my mother's face, it did not look like it was going to be a good story and I instantly regretted my curiosity about the box.

Slowly the uncomfortable feeling began to pervade my bones and circulate through my veins as I stared into my mother's forlorn face. Her eyes were the watery version of the lake at night with a full moon shining upon its glittering surface. "That's alright. I've got homework to do," I told her as I jumped up. Sixteen was too young to find out about anything that had put that kind of a look in my mother's normally radiant eyes; eyes that usually sparkled like a sunrise with the early morning sun.

"Sit down, Marsha." She emphasized her words slowly as if they had been wet mud dredged from the center of the earth. "Sit down, Marsha," she repeated as she sat heavily on the edge of her bed.

Those words again! It wasn't like she'd said, "Sit down dear and have some chocolate cake," or "Sit down dear, I have fifty dollars so you can buy yourself a new dress." Those were the words I would have rather heard but, "Sit down, dear," spoken in that stranger's voice, so unlike her own, suggested she was going to tell me something I didn't want to hear. Reluctantly I sat down, trying unsuccessfully not to look at the box. Perched as it was on the top shelf, it seemed to have grown in size while it sat there; its mystery compounding by each second that passed.

"There are things you should know," she whispered as she lowered her eyes. "Things I haven't told you before." A solitary tear crept slowly down her pale face.

'Oh Gawd,' I thought. 'This is not starting out to be a wonderful conversation.' I mentally kicked myself for having mentioned the box. Words I shouldn't speak have a way of sneaking out of my mouth before I can stop them. "Think before you speak," my mother has always told me. I wished for once I had listened to her wise words but one never knows ahead of time which are the ones to listen to and which are the ones to ignore.

Looking up I saw her dark brown eyes fixed intently on my face. "I should have told you this a long time ago but I've put it off. The fault is mine, darling. Your father has been after me to do so long before now," she said. "I've been afraid. Oh, Gawd," she said as she buried her face in her hands. And although she made no sound, I knew it would only be minutes before her tears would spill over the edges of her cupped hands like water in an overflowing basin.

'Afraid?' I wondered. 'My mother has never been afraid of anything. She is the woman who stood up against bullies when I was eight years old even though her knees were trembling. She is the one who confronted the neighbor when his son stole my bike and, although she hated to make a scene, she marched into the school and talked to the principal when I got detentions for something I didn't do. And she stood up in front of my class when she was petrified to do so and gave a talk about her work because I wanted her to do it for me.'

As I watched my mother trying to battle her fears, I knew it wasn't something I wanted to hear. "Maybe you could tell me later, Mom," I stammered. "If you've waited this long, there's probably no hurry to do it now. I'm sure it can wait." I quickly jumped up and escaping to my own room, closed the door behind me with a dull thud.

My mother did not follow me. She must have agreed with my logic. I breathed a deep sigh of relief as I sunk down onto my bed. I never again mentioned the box on her shelf. Even a nosey and stubborn teenage girl can occasionally learn a lesson or two.

Over the years I had forgotten about the mystery surrounding the box in her closet and life went on pretty much as usual as I grew into young adulthood. That is until my parents' death in a head-on automobile accident when I was twenty-one years old.

Lying quietly in my room later in the day of their memorial service, tears cascaded down my cheeks. Dripping off my chin, the tears ran down my neck as I thought about my parents and remembered my mother's kindness to everyone she came in contact with, the love she had brimming over for family and friends; her compassion, thoughtfulness and consideration. She was cheerful, caring and friendly and always made others feel welcome and loved. My father had possessed the same qualities but in a much quieter way. I never doubted his love for me either with his special smiles meant only for me, treats he'd pick up on his way home from work or the wonderful 'father-daughter' days he'd often plan for the two of us.

I knew I'd been fortunate. I'd had a good life, a happy childhood, parents who loved each other and who loved me and I never felt I'd missed out on anything. I'd had swimming lessons and singing lessons even though I couldn't keep a tune. I'd had ballet lessons even though I had no rhythm and I'd played soccer, to have a balanced life, my parents told me. I'd had art lessons when I'd shown some talent and had gone to gymnastic classes because my best friend went.

The only thing I'd been unhappy about was that I was an only child. "Please, please," I often begged my parents, "can you get me a baby sister?" They'd got me a puppy instead. I had loved the puppy but thought I'd probably have loved a baby sister even more. I'd pointed out that having a sister would mean having a friend for life. They had laughed and said there were many sisters who didn't get along and that my puppy would never argue with me. They may have had a point, he never did.

Now I was all alone, although I still had the dog. When I thought about never seeing either of them again, I felt an emptiness and loneliness like I had never before experienced. What would I do without them? They'd always been there when I needed a shoulder to lean on, they'd been there with an ear to listen, and they were the ones I loved to laugh with.

It was then I remembered the look on my mother's face when I had found the box on the top shelf of her closet. I slowly got up off my bed. The box still sat where I had last seen it. I wondered, 'Did I even want to know what it held?' Probably not. I had a feeling if I looked inside and discovered the secret that lay within, my life would be forever changed. But then I remembered, my life had already changed, it would never be the same again.

My mother was no longer there to confide in, to help me with problems or to just be there when I felt sad. There would be no more father-daughter special occasions and nor would he be there to walk me down the aisle when I got married. There was not even any way to place a phone call to Heaven when I needed to talk. They were gone and I knew my life would be forever changed. My tears ran like a river overflowing its banks.

Through my tears, I stared at the box with mixed emotions, my curiosity slowly growing as I stared at it. Raising my arms, I almost lifted it down before I forced them to my sides. "I won't," I decided firmly forcing myself to go to the kitchen for a cup of tea. 'If I look, it would probably be like eavesdropping when you hear no good said about yourself,' I thought. 'What if it was the same with the box? I'll just leave it, maybe even throw it out,' I decided as I slowly drank my cup of chamomile tea hoping it would bring me the peace and serenity it promised.

As I glanced around, I saw the flowers that filled the living room, their fragrance almost overpowering in the small room. The smell of lilacs, my mother's favorite flowers, almost made me feel nauseous. Putting them on the outside deck, I noticed the sky was becoming a deep royal blue with stars sparkling overhead strewn like jewels upon a velvet robe. The purple and pink sunset had almost disappeared over the horizon but it reminded me of my mother's gentle personality and her sweet smile.

At the table, I thought again about that box on the top shelf. It looked harmless enough but was the secret harmless? It had been serious enough to put that sad look on my mother's face those many years ago. But, I rationalized, it did not appear to be important enough for her to have mentioned it to me again. Could I just throw it away without looking at it? My grandparents had died many years ago and there were no aunts or uncles; only a second cousin, a distant relative of my mother's, who lived so far away that I had only seen her once when I was very small. There was no one else to care what was in that box.

Swallowing the rest of my tea, I walked into my parents' bedroom with a renewed feeling of determination. I lifted the box down, surprised at its weightlessness, and sat on their bed. Staring at it, I willed myself to open it.

As I reached towards the lid, the doorbell rang forcing me to put the box back in the closet. Ellen, my Godmother bustled into the house in her usual excitable fashion. She flung the end of her scarlet-colored scarf over her shoulder before slipping off her elegant jacket, its color reminiscent of newly fallen autumn leaves. "I have been so worried about you being here by yourself, Marsha dear. I came over as soon as I was able to get here. Oh dear," she said as she saw my tear-stained face.

"I'm glad you stopped by," I told her sincerely. "I've been feeling like I've been walloped by life, as if a huge truck has driven over me. I know I was lucky to have had such great parents; but it just doesn't seem fair to lose them both at once." Tears began to slide down my cheeks.

My Godmother put her arms around my shoulders. "Life often isn't fair, dear but they loved you very much, Marsha. You must always remember that." Sitting at the kitchen table with our steaming cups before us, my Godmother smiled, "Is there anything I can help you with, dear? I'm sure there must be a lot to do. You only have to say the word and I will be at your command. That's what Godmothers do, besides looking for charming princes, that is. But unfortunately, princes are in short supply at this time of the year." Her smile, although tinged with sadness, transformed her rather plain face.

"I'm not looking for a prince right now anyway," I said with an attempt at a smile. I thought again of the box in my mother's room. I was not sure whether to mention it to my Godmother or not. Would she know what the box contained?

Aunt Ellen, my mother's very dearest and oldest friend, busied herself around the kitchen cleaning up the dishes left by sympathetic visitors earlier in the day while I sipped my third cup of chamomile tea. It hadn't yet given me the peace and serenity I had hoped for. As I watched Aunt Ellen finish up the dishes and give a last swipe to the counter, I finally made my decision.

"Aunt Ellen, do you know anything about a box my mother had with something in it that perhaps I should know about? Or maybe it isn't important at all and I can just throw it away without opening it," I suggested hopefully.

Drying her hands on a towel, she came to sit at the table. "I do know about the box, dear. I also know that your mother realized she should have told you about it before now. Your father was very upset that you had not been told. But I believe you have a right to know, Marsha. Especially now."

I sat mute. No words fought to escape from my mouth and I could feel my heart pounding erratically, perhaps in warning of what was to come. "I'm not sure I want to know what's in that box."

Aunt Ellen sighed, a sad smile on her face. "You will have to know sooner or later but we won't look at it tonight, my dear. It can wait, it's waited this long. Do you happen to remember your mother's cousin? You haven't seen her since you were about four or five years old. She heard about your mother and father so she's planning to come here tomorrow afternoon for a visit. She feels so badly about your parents. She's alone also. Her parents died some time ago too. She loved your mother very much."

"I sort of remember her. I think I remember that she laughed a lot and was fun. She played with me all the time she was here and brought me a lot of presents. In fact I still have a silver bracelet with my name engraved on it that she gave me. She was quite a bit younger than my mother, I think."

"Yes, she's about fourteen or fifteen years older than you are so she'd be about thirty-five years old or so now. I'm going to pick her up at the airport tomorrow afternoon."

"Does she have anything to do with the box, Aunt Ellen?"

"We won't talk about it right now, dear. You've had an extremely difficult week and I know today particularly has been very hard for you. I think it would be better if we discussed what's in the box tomorrow when you're not so tired. You need to get some rest tonight. After I pick Tonia up at the airport tomorrow, I'll bring her here. We'll all have a nice visit and then we can talk. She's quite anxious to see you again after all these years. She's very fond of you, you know. I've decided that I'm going to stay here with you tonight, dear."

"Just a minute, Aunt Ellen," I called when I heard the doorbell the following afternoon. I quickly dried my hands and with a quick glance in the mirror, I smoothed my flyaway copper colored hair as best as I could. Dabbing a little powder on my hated freckles, I hoped to make a good impression on the only relative I had in the world. I knew it wasn't going to be good as I surveyed my puffy eyes, the green of them barely visible in my swollen face.

Aunt Ellen threw her arms around me, enveloping me in her usual warm embrace. She was dressed in her typical flamboyant style—boots with staggeringly high heels, a leopard print jacket over a long flowing emerald green skirt and a trailing fluorescent green scarf. Her make-up as usual was exaggerated giving her face the look of a cartoon character. She filled the doorway with her presence and I didn't immediately see the small woman standing behind her.

"Marsha, darling," Aunt Ellen gushed as she stepped aside. "This is Tonia. You probably don't remember her—you were so young when she last came for a visit. It's definitely been a long overdue visit, hasn't it? We'll have to make up for that."

The small woman stepped forward with a smile on her face and tears in her eyes. She was about my height with the same golden colored hair. Her eyes, glistening through her tears, were green, and her face was pale with a few freckles scattered across her nose. Dressed in a muted shade of green, she was a frail shadow to Aunt Ellen's bright colors. She stepped forward hesitantly, nerves obvious in the trembling hand she offered me. The shock hit me just before she reached forward to embrace me.

"Come in," I finally managed to stammer as I remembered my manners.

"Sit down, both of you," Aunt Ellen ordered as she bustled about filling the kettle. "I'm going to make us some tea and we'll have some of the donuts I picked up from Tim Hortons. Marsha, why don't you go get the box that your mother had. Maybe now is a good time to look into it."

I looked at Aunt Ellen before my eyes gradually turned to rest on Tonia. Looking at my mother's cousin was like looking into the mirror, right down to the tears cascading down each of our faces. I realized as I watched her hand move forward to gently caress my face that I was no longer interested in the mystery of the box. I suspected I now knew the secret the box on the shelf held.

# THE DIFFERENT FACES
# OF TRUTH

WILLIAM, ROBERT'S BROTHER was fifteen months his junior and he hated him. In fact, he had hated William for as long as he could remember. He had been the pain in the butt who'd followed him everywhere, who didn't have what you could call a brain in his head but who got all the attention. Robert didn't know why because there was nothing loveable about William. Perhaps it was because he was the youngest and the most 'in your face' kind of a person, like a demanding dog. He pestered until he got his way. But why couldn't anyone else see that William was also evil?

Robert remembered scenes from his childhood when his mother would scream in exasperation. "Stop it," she'd yell. Doors would slam as her anger grew to ridiculous proportions. And finally in frustration, "Robert, go to your room."

"What about William? Why doesn't he have to go to his room too?" Robert would say as he turned around to witness the fury of his mother and the inevitable self-satisfied smirk on his brother's face. William was evil.

Somehow they had grown into adulthood but the anger and the hatred he felt towards his brother had continued to escalate as William's behavior toward him became even worse. Robert still didn't understand why William seemed to come out smelling like a bouquet of roses no matter what he did. And based on many of his choices as an adult, he should have been lying in a truck load of skunk cabbages. But that only happened to Robert. It never happened to William.

William had married and divorced young, leaving his wife to raise three small children and his parents holding the bag for his car loan. Robert knew, or at least suspected, that his brother had never paid them back for that loan. During those early years William had irresponsibly bounced from job to job, concerned only with what made him happy and showing little concern for anyone else.

Robert knew all about those days in William's life. He himself had slogged away at his own job and with the responsibility of a new baby and an emotionally unstable wife, he had felt dragged down. William had seemed to be having all the fun yet for Robert, despair never seemed far away.

William had continued to play the carefree bachelor and gone from woman to woman, eventually marrying a second time. Producing two more children in as many years, he had gradually grown tired of marriage again and ran off with his wife's co-worker. At least Robert had heard a rumour to that effect. It had come as no surprise to Robert. With little money, wife number two could not afford to go to court so received little contribution from William towards raising the children.

After another succession of women, he met and married wife number three and fathered three more children. By this time, he had settled down somewhat and had secured himself a well paying job with a future. When he eventually left wife number three for an acquaintance's wife, his ex-wife took him to court and managed to secure reasonable child support. But she hadn't succeeded in getting any of his pension because of some finagling William had done. Robert had heard this from the ex-wife herself so he was fairly sure of the facts.

Wife number four produced no children but when William left, he was richer by half of what she had owned. By wife number five he was picking them carefully based on their financial portfolios, at least that's what it appeared to be because she was pretty well set up Robert knew. After five marriages, he was only paying support for three children and only one had anything to do with him, according to the grape vine.

William now had a well paying secure job with a great pension plan, a home in a nice area, a vacation property, the ability to take a couple of trips each year and all the toys a man could ever want. For all his good fortune, he appeared to give little or nothing to anyone. And to further raise Robert's ire, he was fond of phoning his brother and bragging about what he had and what vacation trips he had taken. It seemed to Robert that as William went through life, the smirk never left his face. Robert's hand twitched uncontrollably when he thought of that smirk.

Robert on the other hand had plodded along. He'd gotten an education, taken a good job and had worked his way up the ladder, step by slow difficult step. It hadn't been easy. Marrying, as it turned out, a non-supportive wife who had produced four rather self-centred children, the product of his wife's doing, he was convinced.

He had worked hard and given his children and his wife his time, his attention and whatever else they had asked for. No matter how much he gave, they wanted more. He continued to give and to give to the point where he was struggling financially. Their hands were constantly out and still he gave more. He was not happy. He struggled through each day with a throb in his head and a constriction in his chest.

He felt unappreciated from the time he woke up in the morning until he went to bed at night. Everyone seemed to take advantage of him. He had worked himself into a position where he was now between a rock and a hard place. If he stopped doing everything, his family would be angry and he felt he would have no one in his life. He couldn't stop now. He sincerely felt that he was doing well by his family because he helped them all and he hoped that one day down the road, they would realize how much he'd done for them. Maybe then, he thought, there would be appreciative responses from them.

When he looked back at the disparity between his and William's treatment as they were growing up and he looked at where he was and where William was and how each had lived their lives so differently, his anger and hatred began to consume and to gnaw at him daily. Depression was never far away, hovering above him waiting to pounce when he least expected it. Life wasn't fair he told himself often. There didn't appear to be any reward in doing good and helping others. Evil seemed to win in this world, he often thought.

Looking at his children he knew he loved them but in moments of honesty and clarity, he could see what they were. They had grown into adulthood becoming lazy, irresponsible and takers. Except for Jenny on whom he concentrated all of his attention, he continued to play the same role of giving with responsibility not being taught or encouraged. It was a cycle that would continue into perpetuity. It was the vicious circle of giving, receiving nothing and feeling that as hard as he tried to win favor and love, it continued to elude him and to turn sour on him. History was repeating itself, he often thought, 'And I'm always going to be the loser.' Each time Robert puzzled over this, he could never determine why this was the case.

"Dad, we can't make our mortgage payment this month. We'll need you to pay it for us," Robert's eldest daughter informed him. He looked at her hands, fresh from the manicurist, and her hair, obviously professionally done and remembered this was the third time in almost as many months that she had expected him to pay it for them. Annoyance, followed by anger began to worm its way into his thoughts. He knew after he'd paid it, fury would consume him next. But, he thought, what could he do? He couldn't let them lose the house. After all, he'd helped them with the down payment so they could get their first home. He didn't want them to lose their house although he doubted, in his more depressed moments, that he'd ever see the money he'd invested returned to him.

"This will have to be the last time, Sharon," he told her. "I'm not made of money."

"Sure, Pops," Sharon called as she opened the door and left without a backward glance or a thank you.

Robert watched her walk to her new Honda Pilot parked in his driveway. He couldn't help noticing that her clothes never looked like she shopped at Zellers or WalMart either. Sitting in his worn-out recliner that he'd repaired in a couple of places with duct tape, he halfheartedly flipped through the channels, his anger increasing as he did.

'And William,' he thought, 'sitting on his fancy furniture in his nice house—he doesn't deserve everything he has. What does he do for his kids? He didn't even pay for their university education. They had to pay for it themselves. And they had to get their own cars too.' Robert refused to think about the good jobs some of William's children had compared to his own children. Robert's children had shown no inclination towards going to University or even in finishing high school. And they weren't exactly interested in keeping steady jobs either unfortunately, but he was unprepared to admit that. 'I'll just have to keep helping them until they get on their feet,' he sighed. 'That's what parents do when they love their children. Damn William, he doesn't deserve to live such a charmed life.'

Halfway through Survivor, Robert's phone rang. He was tempted to just let it ring because it usually only ever rang when someone wanted something. 'Aw Hell,' he thought as he reached over for the receiver, 'I know I'll end up helping them anyway.' "Hello," he answered in an anger roughened voice.

"Dad, I was hoping you were going to be home. My car has been making all sorts of noises for the last couple of weeks and now it's finally given up," Melissa, Robert's second oldest daughter said.

"What do you mean it gave up? Have you been taking it for oil changes like I told you to?"

"I can't afford oil changes, you know that. And I've got to have money for a social life, you know. But I don't know how I'm going to get to work tomorrow, or home again, for that matter. Can I take your car?"

"I have to drive your brother Michael to work since he got his license suspended and you know I drive Jarrod to school every day. Your work isn't very far, you could walk there in five minutes."

"I'm not going to walk to work. Can you imagine what my hair would look like by the time I got there in this weather. Why can't Jarrod take his bike to school? And why are you driving Jarrod to school every day anyway?" Melissa whined.

"There's still Michael to get to work. I can't be everywhere at once," Robert said ignoring her questions. He could feel the pressure begin to build inside his head.

"It was Michael's fault he lost his license. That's the third time he's been caught drinking and driving. Well then, can you buy me another car. I have to get back and forth to work unless you want me to just quit my job."

"And how will you support yourself?" Robert said as he tried to control his rising anger.

"I'll move in with you and let you spoil me like you do Jarrod and Michael."

"You're all spoiled. I do things for all of you. You should have a father like your Uncle William and then you'd get nothing done for you."

"Dad, we're all so sick of hearing about how worse off you are than Uncle William. He has a nice house and his kids have gone to University—well Jaycee and Marcie have anyway."

"Your Uncle William didn't pay for their education; they had to pay for it themselves. I'd have been quite willing to pay for all of you to go to University but none of you wanted to go. And they grew up having to have part-time jobs to pay for any extras they wanted."

"I don't care what they had to do. Can you get me another car? I don't have all the nice things like Sharon does either. Her husband is always getting her things."

'And I'm doing it too,' Robert thought as he remembered the last three mortgage payments he had paid for Sharon and John. He felt the guilt as it began to pervade his thoughts. "Okay, I'll get you another car but it won't be expensive and you'll have to look after it."

"Good. Can we go look tomorrow? I'll take the day off."

"You seem to take a lot of time off work, Melissa. Do they pay you for all the days you take off? Are you getting your credit cards paid down, by the way?"

"Uh, sure. Can we go tomorrow?"

After Robert had hung up the phone, he went to the side bar and poured himself a scotch over ice. Sipping it slowly, he kept his eyes on Survivor and watched the leaders of each tribe. The leader of the one tribe reminded him of William—manipulative and sneaky—pretending to be one way when he actually was quite different than he appeared to be. Robert quickly developed an aversion to him and turned his attention to the leader of the opposing tribe.

As that leader tried to help each of the members and tried to get along with each of them, the inevitable behind-the-scenes backstabbing was beginning. An alliance was being formed to get him off the island and out of the game. They thought he might be able to outwit them in some of the games. Another alliance that was being formed felt he might be useful for the time being because he was a hard worker and they wanted to keep him because they weren't prepared to work hard themselves. He could see the similarities between himself and the leader of the second tribe. Good never wins.

He got up to get himself another drink of scotch. Like life, he thought as he watched the two leaders battle for positions in their tribes, appreciation and admiration are in short supply. He drained his glass in a single gulp and reached again for the bottle. But before he could pour himself another drink, the phone rang again.

"Hi there, Bro. I thought I'd let you know that we're leaving for Arizona in a few days," William said. Robert could hear the smile in his voice and could imagine the usual smirk on his brother's face.

"Again, heh? You're away more than you're here," Robert said bitterly.

"No. We can't be away more than six months each year but it's always much less than that, three months at the most usually. I'm still working but I've been fortunate in being able to cut back on my hours. We'll be down there this time for about a month. Why don't you come down and visit—stay with us for a while. We could get some golfing in. It would do you good to get away."

"I don't think so. Some of us have responsibilities. Not all of us can traipse all over the country as if we don't have a care in the world."

"I don't know why I can't Robert. My kids are all grown and doing well for themselves. Your kids are grown too, Bro. I think you need to relax, swim in the pool and enjoy the sunshine."

"What about your grandchildren? I don't understand you, William. You just run off every year and leave your family. You're never here for them."

"For one thing I'm here much more than I'm away. But regarding the grandchildren, their parents look after them and if anyone needs me when I'm away, they certainly know where they can reach me. And they know I can be home in a few hours time. I think the only one who begrudges me the time I spend away is you, Robert. I've never been able to figure out what your problem is."

"I don't have a problem, William and I don't begrudge you anything. But to me my family is very important and I couldn't spend the time away from them that you do."

"It would probably do both them and you good to go away for awhile. From what I've seen over the years, your children seem to take advantage of you. It's one thing to be available to help but it's quite another matter when they take advantage of you. Anyway, think about it Robert. You're always welcome to come and stay with us in Arizona any time. But we also wanted to invite you over for dinner before we leave. Tomorrow evening, if you're available?"

'Yes,' Robert thought as he slowly hung up the phone, 'so he can gloat about what he has and I don't have.' But it was William's last remark before he hung up that particularly rankled him. The gall of William, he thought, to say that hatred and resentment can make an evil man out of the best. 'As if he knows anything about being a good person.' He could feel the heat in his face as his blood pressure rose to soaring heights. Pouring another glass of scotch over ice, he sat back in his chair. Survivor was over but there was a fight being waged in his own living room. He didn't have to worry about being able to build a fire in order to survive; one was going on right within himself.

As Robert drank his scotch he thought about how selfish William was for going away for long periods of time and not being around to help out his children. They always had to depend on themselves; they knew they couldn't count on their father. He tried to push out of his mind a remark William had made some time ago about his own children. He had said they were adults and of course they depended on themselves because he had raised them to be responsible. And the most irritating remark of all was when he had implied that because they had been raised to be responsible, they had also learned good work ethics so had no problem hanging onto their jobs.

'What had he meant by that?' Robert fumed as he thought about that conversation. His children were unfortunate that they'd had some very lousy bosses. If they'd had decent bosses, they could have hung onto their jobs too. Robert knew very well what William's implication was. It was like all of his remarks—that everything he had and everything he did was better than Robert's. 'Well Brother,' he thought, 'you should conquer your own evils before you begin to judge me.'

As Robert allowed his anger to consume him, a conversation he'd had with his ex-wife came back to haunt him as well. "Robert," she had said, "nothing is all bad and nothing is all good. But to you, everything is either all black or all white. Life is filled with greys too. No one can live a totally black and white world, not even you. In the process of fighting the evil you think is in William, you may become evil yourself while you let your hatred, your resentment and your anger fester inside of you. And although you may wear the mask of good, I know there's an evil growing in your soul. I can see it every time your temper explodes."

He remembered how angry he had been with her at the time and had automatically lumped her in with the William's of the world. Marion had always judged him too. From morning until night she had criticized and then complained and finally she had left him for someone who admitted that although he felt he was a nice person, he knew that like everyone else, he was not perfect. That paragon of goodness apparently admitted he made mistakes which, Marion was quick to point out, her husband never was capable of doing.

"I was surprised you decided to come for dinner, Robert. When I talked to you it didn't sound like you were going to be able to make it.

I'm glad you did," William smiled at his brother. And when William smiled, Robert didn't miss the smirk behind the smile.

"We're having rack of lamb. Elaine does a fabulous job of cooking it. Not everyone can. I hope you enjoy it."

"I'm not surprised she would do it well. She does everything well, doesn't she?"

William looked at Robert wondering at the meaning behind his words. He never knew with Robert. "What have you been doing lately? We don't get a chance to talk very often," William said.

"No, we don't. I'm quite busy with my family. I like to be involved with my children," Robert said with a half chuckle.

"Yes, I know you do. Oh excuse me please, I'll just grab the phone." Robert watched his brother while he talked then putting his hand over the phone William called, "Elaine, Marcie wants to know if we would like to come over for dinner tomorrow night. Jaycee will be there too."

"That would be lovely but explain that we'll have to make it an early night. The next day is going to be pretty busy."

Robert looked around at his brother's home. The living room furniture must have set him back at least twelve grand and the dining room, he shook his head, he couldn't even imagine the cost of it. 'How can he do it when he's had so many wives?' he wondered angrily. 'And the phone call, what a crock that is.' From what he'd heard, there was no relationship between William and his children. Robert refused to think about the few invitations he'd had to dinner from his own children, mostly to soften him before they hit him up for money, he reluctantly had to admit to himself. But usually they didn't even make that token effort. But why was he even thinking about that now, he wondered as he looked out the window at the beautiful view that lay before him.

He heard a sound behind him and turned around. "Lovely view, isn't it?" William said. "Can I get you a drink, Robert?"

'Ah, the bragging. It never stops,' Robert thought. "Uh, no, no thank you. I don't really drink much anymore."

William nodded as he went over to pour himself a glass of wine. "No? We usually have a drink before dinner and then one with our meal. I hope you're hungry. Do the children have you over very often for dinner?"

'Uh, a dig and then a quick turn of the knife. William knows how to do it well,' Robert thought angrily. "Now and again but everyone's so busy rushing to games and lessons." Robert turned again to look at the view. The lights of the city sparkled in the distance. "I would think you'd miss all of this in Arizona."

"Arizona has its own unique beauty. There really is something quite beautiful about the desert, a restfulness that's hard to find anywhere else. And sunsets on the desert are unbelievable although you have to enjoy them when you can because they're gone very quickly."

'Of course, more bragging. And why not? That's all William knows how to do.'

"So I've heard. Well, when my children are all set up then I can begin to think about me."

"Robert, I hate to remind you but your youngest is twenty-five years old. You're starting to look after your grandchildren now. When are you going to take time for yourself? I think that time is long past. Don't you ever just feel like packing it up and going someplace to get away? I really would like you to visit us in Arizona."

"I hardly think I'll be taking advise from you, Mr. Responsibility. I enjoy doing things for my children and yes, my grandchildren too. And they appreciate everything I do for them—it makes me feel good." The lie rolled off his tongue without thought as he concentrated his anger on William's arrogance.

"As long as you're happy, Robert. That's the main thing. But I can't help wondering why you always seem so angry with me. This has been going on for years and I've never understood why. Could you tell me and then maybe I could rectify what it is I'm doing wrong."

"I can't believe you don't get it, William." Robert glimpsed Elaine standing at the kitchen doorway with a frown on her attractive face. 'And that was another thing—how did William always attract such good looking women?'

"I'm sorry, I don't. Could you enlighten me?"

"Dear brother, I would love to. You are evil and yet everything falls into your lap. You lead a charmed life and you don't deserve it." Robert heard Elaine's loud gasp. 'She'll know what kind of a person she married when I get through,' Robert thought with an inward grin.

"I'd like to hear about this charmed life you think I've lead, Robert. Go ahead."

"Well first, you leave your first wife and three children for someone else." Robert could feel the heat begin to color his face.

"Actually Robert, she left me for someone else. I came home to a note and very little else left in the house. The biggest thing I had left was the mortgage payment."

"Well, you left Mom and Dad to pay for your car loan."

"I will admit that for a while they did pay it until I could get the house sold because the mortgage payment was eating me alive. But I paid them back every cent and paid off all the rest of the bills as well. After that I was still in the hole and for several years the hole kept getting bigger. Wife number one was quite a spender. My mistake was in marrying so young. Twenty is too young to get married."

"And wife number two, what about her? You left her with two children and, I heard, no support."

"Where did you hear that from, Robert? Did she also tell you she was gay and that she decided to go with her true feelings? The decision to leave was hers alone. As for the children, I did pay some support but I wasn't making a lot of money and there were now five children to support. There wasn't an awful lot to spread around but she did get what I could afford."

Robert glanced over to where Elaine stood. He felt his confidence sag somewhat when he saw the angry expression on her face. 'Is she mad at me?' he thought with some surprise. 'Why me? I haven't done anything wrong. And I don't believe a word William is saying.'

"Uh, what about wife number three and those children?"

"I'm sure you've heard stories about that as well. Stories you could have asked me about yourself instead of believing the worst about me, Robert. I could harbor some anger myself if I wanted to because you have chosen to believe other people's lies against the only brother you have. As for wife number three, as you put it, the split was mutual and it's unimportant at this time what the reasons for it were."

"I knew her and I know the reason and if I were you Robert, I wouldn't be holding your brother responsible for that break-up," Elaine suddenly spoke, anger making her normally quiet voice sound harsh in the quiet room.

"It doesn't matter, Elaine. Robert has always had opinions about me that he has held onto tightly. In answer to your question, I was making more money then so I was also able to pay support for them as well. I'm very close to the children, especially Jaycee and Marcie. Meredith is more like her mother. In those days a father didn't have a chance of getting custody. If I could have, I would have tried."

"What about your pension money?"

A sad smile crossed William's face. "Ah, she even mentioned that. Did she by any chance tell you that I cashed it in to pay for Marcie's and Jaycee's university? She wanted it for herself rather than use it for the girls' education. She was very angry about that. And before you ask, wife number four and I were never compatible; it was a mistake right from the beginning that we both agreed upon. I will admit Robert, that I have made many mistakes, although not as many as you seem to think I have. And I will no doubt continue to make mistakes; we all do, that's life, it's part of being human. And I think being able to admit our mistakes helps to make us more human also. I will admit that I haven't chosen my wives well. That is until Elaine and she's the one that chose me. I had decided never to marry again. I'm very fortunate that Elaine had other ideas."

"And before you ask about me, since I'm wife number five, I want to tell you that William is a good husband, a good man. He has made me very happy. He's a cheerful, optimistic person; not moody or morose all the time. I couldn't imagine living with someone who was always depressed and angry, seeing the worst in others."

Robert squirmed under her direct gaze. "I suppose that last remark is directed at me," he replied.

"I think we should drop the conversation now, Robert before things may be said that can't be taken back. I have answered your questions, questions that shouldn't have been asked in the first place but I've answered them in good spirit. I hope from now on we can have a better relationship. If there is anything else bothering you, please say without letting it fester in you. It would be nice if we could have a relationship that isn't based on anger."

Robert turned to look out at the view again. Looking at the stars sparkling in the sky and the full moon creating a swath of light across the water's surface, he could feel some of the tension drain from his body. The city's lights glittering on the horizon completed the feeling. There was still some residual angry feelings towards William; there may always be, he'd lived with it for such a long time. But his main anger was more directed towards his children. But whose fault was it?

Theirs? His? Was he a blamer? Was he unwilling to take responsibility for his part in making his children what they were?

"Dinner is ready," Elaine called. "Come and sit down."

Robert felt the weight of William's hand on his shoulder. He hadn't known his brother had been standing behind him.

"Come on, let's have dinner, Bro," William said as he preceded his brother to the well-laid table.

"This lamb is great," Robert said as he picked up his napkin and dabbed at his chin.

"I wasn't bragging. I truly believe Elaine cooks a great meal."

Robert felt twinges of jealousy as he saw the smile that passed between William and his wife. He saw genuine love reflected on their faces when they looked at each other. 'Who knows,' Robert thought, 'maybe this marriage will last.' Who was he to talk he realized when his marriage hadn't lasted either. The thing that made him different from his brother was that he didn't keep on trying but then William seemed to be more optimistic by nature. One kick at the can was enough as far as he was concerned. 'But who knows . . . '

"You seem very quiet, Robert. Is everything alright?" Elaine asked. "Can I get you anything?"

"No thanks, I'm fine. I'm just enjoying your lovely rack of lamb. And I'm not even a lamb lover, or so I thought. When did you say you were leaving?"

"On Thursday. Two days from now. I certainly hope you decide to come down for a visit. I think you'd enjoy yourself," William smiled. Robert noticed that the smirk seemed to have disappeared from his brother's face. 'Strange,' he thought.

"I'll consider it. I'll see how things work out but it certainly sounds tempting."

When Robert later thought back on his visit with William, he shook his head. If William had been telling the truth, he had certainly misjudged his brother. He had to admit that he had enjoyed the meal and the evening with both of them. 'Heck, I deserve a trip,' he thought when he remembered their invitation to Arizona. 'But . . .' there always seemed to be buts, he realized. 'I think it's time I did something to set matters straight with my children.'

"Hello Michael, how much longer is your driving suspension?"

"Another month. I think four months was pretty harsh. It wasn't like I was falling down drunk. I was just a little bit over the limit," Michael grumbled.

"Well, I have received an invitation to go to Arizona for a couple of weeks. I'll drive you to work for one more week and then you'll have to make other arrangements for the next two weeks while I'm gone. And Michael, this has been the fourth time you've lost your license—if you lose it again, I will not drive you to work. You'll have to come up with another alternative."

"What? Why are you doing this?" Michael demanded.

"Because I think at twenty-nine years of age you are old enough to take responsibility for your own actions. You didn't learn before because you weren't inconvenienced. You had a built-in chauffeur. I won't be your chauffeur again."

"I don't know what you're talking about, not being inconvenienced. It cut into my social life. I think you're being incredibly selfish, just thinking about a trip for yourself."

"But you have only yourself to blame, Michael. Anyway I'm not arguing with you. You'll have to make other arrangements for those two weeks and that's it. And I'm going to add, if you can't talk to me in a civil manner you can forget rides for this week also. Talking about selfish, I don't recall any appreciation being shown by you."

"Appreciation? You're my father! I think that's what you're expected to do." Michael's voice was beginning to get the hard edge to it that Robert recognized.

"Not when you're twenty-nine years old. You are way past the age of needing someone to look after you. At least you should be able to look after your own problems by now. I'm actually doing you a favor, Michael, finally. I'm teaching you about responsibility. If you want me to continue to drive you this week, let me know."

Robert could almost hear the wheels turning in his son's head before he spoke again. "I'll need you to drive me," he muttered before he abruptly hung up the phone.

'Well,' Robert thought, 'no appreciation there. Now for Jarrod.'

"Hello, Sharon. I'm going away for a few weeks and won't be able to drive Jarrod to school so either you or John will have to. I'm not quite sure how it got to be my job every day anyway."

"I can't drive him. I'm not up by the time he leaves for school and John leaves early every day," Sharon whined. "You offered to do it, Pops. Do you want him to walk to school now?"

"I offered to do it when he was younger. I wasn't planning on doing it for the rest of my life. But I know what you could do. You could get up and drive him; he is after all your son, your only child I might add. So I will leave that decision up to you, Sharon."

"You must be getting senile in your old age, Pops, otherwise you'd never let Jarrod walk to school by himself. He'll be wet and cold by the time he gets there."

"I think since he's your child the responsibility is yours because I know I'm going to Arizona. I think it's time you learned to be responsible. And I'm reminding you that the last money I gave you for the mortgage is the last money I will be giving you. You and John will have to decide how you are going to manage to pay it. You may have to cut back in other ways or you, Sharon, may have to get a job."

"I don't get you, Pops. You sound like you woke up on the wrong side of the bed this morning. Maybe you better go back and try getting up again. I don't like being talked to like that, not even by my father," Sharon's voice was beginning to sound petulant. Robert remembered that she had always sounded like that when she was a teenager. He realized suddenly, she had never grown up. She was still expecting her father would do everything for her.

'Well, that's going to stop right now,' Robert thought. 'What an eye-opener this has been.'

Robert laughed halfheartedly. "I've just had my eyes opened, Sharon and I thank you for that. And I've suddenly realized that with everything I've done for all of you, not one of you appreciates a thing. You are all selfish and ungrateful."

Robert heard the phone bang in his ear and he slowly hung up. He wasn't sure how he felt but he'd begun the process so he decided he might as well wait to see where the pieces fell. He was beginning to realize that they had to learn to be responsible for themselves and for their actions or they'd be dependent upon him their whole lives.

"Melissa, how are you? I'm going away to Arizona for a couple of weeks. I just wanted to remind you that you are responsible for your own car and if you don't look after it, I won't be buying you another one."

"I told you I would, Dad. Have you talked to Jenny?"

"No, why?"

"I think she's in trouble. But she wouldn't tell me what it's about. I told her to call you but she said she didn't want to bother you because you had so many problems already."

Robert's heart dropped like a boulder into the pit of his stomach. Jenny was the one he had pinned all of his hopes on. She was the shining star amongst his offspring. "I'll call her. Thanks for letting me know, Melissa."

"Jenny?" When she answered, his daughter's voice sounded small as it floated across the telephone wires. He saw her as she had been as a child, her blonde curls circling her head like a halo. "I was talking to Melissa. She said I should give you a call; that you might want to talk to me."

"Oh, Dad, I'm so sorry." Robert could hear the tears in his daughter's voice. She was the one who had never asked him for anything and his heart broke at the sound of her tears.

"What is it, Jenny?" Robert could hear his youngest daughter sniffing in an effort to control her emotions.

"I don't know what to do. I'm . . . going to . . . have a baby, Dad."

Jenny's tears had escalated and Robert didn't know what to say. "A . . . baby?" he stammered.

"I don't want to . . . get an . . . abortion. I could never do that."

"Can you come over here? We'll discuss what your options are, Honey."

After Robert had hung up the phone, he poured himself a glass of scotch. Thinking about what Jenny had told him, he realized that this was worse than buying a new car or paying Sharon's mortgage payment. This could mean a lifetime of helping. Reaching for the phone, he called his ex-wife, Marion. "Have you talked to Jenny lately?"

"I talked to her yesterday. She sounded rather subdued but when I asked, she said everything was fine."

"Well, things aren't alright. I just found out she's pregnant. She's on her way over here now so we can discuss her options although she told me that abortion isn't one of them."

"Pregnant? Well, I don't blame her for not wanting to get an abortion. But she's certainly not in a position to raise a child by herself either. She's too young."

"Not really when you consider it. You were twenty-five when Sharon was born. I just called to find out if you wanted to be part of the conversation, Marion."

"Well Robert, this is a first. You've always been the one with all the answers. Never mind. Yes, I'll be there shortly."

Robert finished his drink with a gulp when the doorbell rang. "Jenny, you got here quickly. Come on in, dear. I've asked your mother to join us. She'll be here shortly."

As Jenny sat down in her favourite chair, Robert realized how thin she was. Although her face still bore the signs of the tears she had shed, she looked fairly calm. With Robert's new thinking, he realized his daughter was probably going to be even more unhappy with his recent decision to change his life. Robert had decided that he would be supportive and he would help but he was not going to take responsibility. Jenny would have to bear the burden of responsibility herself. She was going to have some consequences and she wasn't going to like it. It broke Robert's heart but he had to do it or he'd be raising another child for the rest of his life.

"How far along are you, Jenny?"

"Just over two months. I just found out yesterday. I told Todd. He got quite upset. You'd have thought I did this all by myself. He left and I haven't heard from him since."

"I gather then that he doesn't want to get married." Robert looked inquiringly at Jenny.

"I would never marry him now anyway. He doesn't want to accept any responsibility at all. I can see now how immature he is."

"We're going to talk about responsibility, Jenny. And I think he's going to have to take his share of the responsibility whether he wants to or not. Now you said abortion was not an option?"

Robert watched his daughter fiercely shake her head. "Have you thought about giving the baby up for adoption?"

"No," Jenny's face had blanched at the thought. "I'll think of something, but not that."

"Okay, we know what are not options. Now we have to work on solutions. Oh, there's your mother now," Robert said as the doorbell rang.

Marion leaned over and hugged her daughter, wiping the tears from her face as she did so while Robert filled her in on their conversation. "We'll work something out," Marion said as she smiled at her daughter.

"First of all, if Todd isn't prepared to pay child support willingly, you'll have to take him to Court. That will be his responsibility. And you make good money, Jenny so you'll have to save as much as you can between now and when you have your baby. You'll be off work for some time after your baby is born. I will be supportive and will help but you are going to have to remember that you are going to have to take responsibility for the raising of your baby. It's a lot of responsibility, Jenny. What do you think, Marion?"

Robert noticed that Marion was startled by his answer. 'Of course,' he thought, 'she doesn't know the decision I've made.'

"I think you've changed. What happened?"

"This isn't about me, Marion. What do you have to say, Jenny?"

"I agree. I fully intended to take responsibility. It has always bothered me that the rest of the family have been such takers and have never appreciated anything you've done for them and I know you've done a lot. I was determined that I was not going to take anything from you."

"Well, the rest of the family are not going to take advantage of me any longer either. It's going to stop. It was the lack of appreciation that bothered me the most. I know you've never asked for anything. What ideas have you got?"

Jenny looked from her mother to her father. "I've been thinking about it a lot since I found out. I will work as long as I can and save money. I'm going to look for a cheaper place to live. If I can afford to, I'd like to take a year maternity leave before I go back to work again. In the meantime that will give me time to find a good daycare. I've heard that it's hard to find daycare places for babies. I should be able to make it even though I know it's not going to be easy. But I'm determined. I really do want to keep this baby."

"I've got that downstairs suite. My tenant just moved out last week. You could move in there if you wanted to," Marion said. "I'd have to charge you something but it would be less than you'd have to pay anywhere else. And you would have your own privacy. That way I could help you occasionally with babysitting. Not all the time, mind you."

"And I'll help you however I can too," Robert smiled.

Jenny's eyes slowly filled with tears as she smiled at her parents. "Thank you so much. I was so afraid to tell you. I wanted to think of a solution first but you've both helped me. Thank you." Getting up she gave each of her parents a hug.

As Robert watched his daughter go out the door, he felt proud of her. He wasn't happy but he was pleased that she had come up with her own solution and hadn't asked for anything. He glanced at his ex-wife who was looking at him with a strange expression on her face. He realized belatedly that she was wearing her hair differently and it was becoming. When had she done that? And she'd lost some weight. He had to admit to himself that she really looked quite nice.

Marion suddenly smiled at her husband. "Robert, let's sit down and have a talk. It's been a long time. Are you going to offer me a drink?"

# A LAMB'S TALE

LYNNE REMEMBERED THE day, as if it had just happened, when they had joined the 4-H Lamb Club in their rural area. Her brother, Rich, just over a year her senior, had bounced around their parent's small farm in his protracted excitement. She, being of a more refined temperament, but just as excited, quietly stated that she was going to 'Make the Best Better' for their club, community, country and world.

They knew the motto backwards and forwards chanting it at 4-H Club gatherings and hopping from foot to foot in their eagerness to return home to care for their lambs. Both children were consumed with love for these fluffy little creatures as they curried and brushed, fed and watered and cleaned up after them.

Lynne believed that her white-faced lamb was the most beautiful one in the world although she did admit, under pressure, that her brother's black-faced lamb came in a pretty close second.

At the tender age of ten, Lynne's maternal instincts were already full-blown as she shed tears when tails were docked and ears were tagged. And when the shears were placed in her small hands for her first lesson in shearing, the tears crept silently down her pale face. "What if he gets cut?" she asked. "And he bleeds? And then he dies? I would just have to die too. Why can't we just leave him nice and fluffy, like this?"

Rich, not having an ounce of maternal instinct, enjoyed everything involving the grooming and caring of his lamb. Tail-docking time was an adventure to him, as was the ear tagging. And making a halter from a length of rope was another wonderful and useful thing to learn, he believed. He knew that this was truly his road to the future. When he grew up, he decided, he would own a whole barnyard full of black-faced lambs.

As the annual Fall Fair approached, care of the lambs escalated to a frenzied level. No two lambs ever knew such devoted love before. During the judging competitions, as Lynne stood with her lamb by her side at one end of the row, she looked down the line at her brother standing at the opposite end.

"Judging of lambs is based on eye appeal initially," the judge told the exhibitors. "But they must also have a good degree of muscling, balance and style, soundness and structural correctness. The loin and rump should make up one-third of the lamb's total body length and the lambs should have good thickness through the leg area as well. We also look for straightness of lines. Your part is important as well," he told them. "It's important how they stand; you'll have to set their feet and it'll help if you talk quietly to your lamb. The best of luck to all of you."

"My lamb is the fairest of them all," Lynne told her brother with not a little hint of pride following the judging. "Look at all the ribbons he got."

"Uhmm," he smirked. "Don't you know why he was winning? He's winning for his meat value. It means that people are going to eat him."

"No they're not. I won't let anyone eat him. Daddy won't let them," Lynne yelled as she raced off to where her lamb was contentedly chewing a few tufts of remaining grass in the muddy enclosure.

"You're just saying that, Rich."

As the next big judging event that all 4-H'ers eagerly looked forward to drew near, Rich asked his sister, "Are you going to take your lamb to the Pacific National Exhibition? It's supposed to be guaranteed fun. But I think you might be too young 'cause you still play with dolls. The other kids would tease you."

"I'm not too young," Lynne said as the tears spilled down her cheeks. "Daddy said he would think about letting me go too. He said that we'll be staying in dormitories, eating in a cafeteria and meeting other kids from all over the province. He said we'll meet people that we'll know for years and he thought it might be good for me. He'll let me go, I know he will."

"But you'll be the youngest, and probably the quietest and maybe even the loneliness. I don't think you'd have a very good time."

"Won't you stay with me?"

"The boys will be staying somewhere different than the girls and besides, I'll be doing 4-H Club stuff. I'll be pledging my head to clearer thinking; my heart to greater loyalty; my hands to larger service and my health to better living. I'll be busy doing guy stuff."

"But what about me? I can do that too. I don't want to be all alone."

"Then why don't you stay home or maybe you could play with the girls if you do go. I think it'll be a mistake though."

"I don't want to stay home but I don't know any of the other girls. This is the biggest event of the whole summer, Rich. I can't just stay home and miss it. I know, you don't want me to go because you want to win all the ribbons," she said as she spun around to face him, suddenly realizing the reason for his objections. "I know you think your black-faced lamb is better than mine." Placing her hands on her hips, she said, "I'm going to go."

"I know mine is better; he's one of the elite. Everywhere you look there are white lambs. So what do you think makes yours so special, Lynne?" Rich turned his back on his sister as he continued to curry his lamb.

"He's just better, that's all," she said as she flounced off in the direction of the house.

Appealing to a higher authority, Lynne eventually received permission to attend the Pacific National Exhibition and, while happy to be included, was forced to live under the barely restrained resentment of her older brother. That is, until his lamb began to start winning ribbons.

Watching in confusion as each blue ribbon was pinned onto Rich's black-faced lamb, Lynne realized she wasn't having much fun at what was supposed to be a guaranteed fun experience. Following at a distance behind her brother as he laughed and ran with other boys his age, she shyly watched the girls, all older and more worldly. They were all beginning to wear make-up and their first training bras while she sat on a bench at the logging exhibit looking like a small boy with a ponytail.

Finally, for lack of something better to do, she mucked out the barns because she seemed to be the only one available to do it and at least she could talk to the animals. She was comfortable with them, they were no more worldly than she was. At meal times, hurrying from the barns, she was always the last one into the cafeteria. Forced to sit at a table by herself where there was no chatter or laughter, her brother pretended not to know her. Later when the older children laughed and played 'Truth or Dare', she sat on the sidelines because she was too shy to be part of the group. As the week progressed Lynne grew more upset and unhappy, further exasperated by the fact that no ribbons lined her beautiful lamb's stall. And by the end of the week, she had the only pillow in the dormitory that was stained and dampened with tears. But the one positive light in the misery of her week was the hope that maybe now, her lamb would not be the first on someone's dinner table.

Lynne was crestfallen after her return from the Pacific National Exhibition. Rich accused her of being jealous but she knew that wasn't true. It wasn't because of the ribbons. The whole experience had been demoralizing. She realized that her brother had been right. She hadn't fit in with the other girls; she had been too young to go. As she'd watched the older girls, she felt younger and more insecure than she had ever felt in all her days of going to school.

While she leaned on the fence, thinking her deep thoughts, she watched her lamb walk lazily towards the salt block. When she'd been working in the barns she'd heard a lot of talking between other 4-H'ers. She realized now that the judges determined the winning lambs based on, like Rich said, their meat value but also on their potential to be good breeding stock. She knew they also classified their wool.

Lynne thought about the fact that her lamb was a Suffolk. They were considered to be excellent market lambs, so she knew the judges would be looking for what basically constituted a good lamb chop. One of the older boys in the barn had said that the heavy muscled lambs have the highest ranking although they didn't want them to be too fat. He said they also looked at their carcass merit. Lynne had almost gagged when she heard that gem of wisdom. He also said that when people buy market lambs they like them to be between ninety and one hundred and ten pounds. 'Maybe,' she thought hopefully, 'I could put him on a diet.'

"Are you taking your lamb to auction after all the competitions?" the boy had asked Lynne.

"The auction?" She knew as she stood there that bewilderment and fear had shone brightly from her ten year old face. "I . . . ah . . . don't think so."

"Most of the lambs here will go to auction because most of them were judged as market lambs. Your brother's lamb won in the breeding category though so he'll probably get more money for his. Although it all depends on who is at the market that day. It's like everything else, supply and demand.

'Great,' Lynne thought as she watched her lamb leisurely lick from the salt block before meandering over to the water trough. She had probably taken better care of her lamb than she should have, she thought. Now he fit right into the category of being excellent rack of lamb. Lynne had heard her parents rave about a good rack of lamb but hadn't thought about it in terms of her own lamb. "What can I do?" she cried.

"What are you doing?" Rich asked as he came up behind her. "You're not still upset about the exhibition and not winning any ribbons, are you?"

"No. Are you going to sell your lamb at the auction?"

"Where did you get a stupid idea like that. I'm keeping him," Rich said. "You sure come up with some loony ideas sometimes."

"It's not my idea. One of the bigger boys at the barns said that's what happens to them after the competitions are over. He said they either get sold to the market where . . ." Tears began to cascade down Lynne's cheeks and she wiped her nose with the back of her hand.

"Well, mine isn't going to be sold," Rich's angry voice swirled around Lynne's head.

"Mine isn't going to be sold either," Lynne answered with as much vehemence as her brother. "No one is going to take him," she added to further reinforce her stand. Rich made no reply but stalked deliberately toward the house.

Lynne gave her lamb a hug and slowly followed her brother. As she came in the door, she could hear her father's soft voice explaining, "That's usually what happens, Rich. Then in the Spring you get another lamb to raise which you'll show at competitions next year. That's what life on a farm is like. If we kept every animal that was ever born on this farm, we couldn't afford to feed them all or have time to look after them. This is a working farm, son. It's not a hobby farm."

"But I want to keep him," Rich insisted stubbornly.

"Son, this isn't a sheep farm. We're dairy farmers. And you know we sell a lot of the calves once they're ready for auction."

"That's different. I didn't raise them and look after them. I don't even know them."

"Your lamb will go to a good breeder and he'll be well looked after. I know most of the breeders around here. Maybe you could even visit him occasionally," his father said as he placed his hand on his son's shoulder.

"And I'm not going to sell mine either," Lynne said. Tears flowed unchecked down her face. "I don't want him to be a lamb chop or rack of lamb."

Lynne's father smiled sadly at his daughter. "Yes, I'll admit that yours is a different matter. He would very likely be bought for the market. But think about when you're eating a steak or even having a hamburger. Where do you think that meat comes from?"

"Yuck, I don't ever want to eat another hamburger again. How can people be so cruel? I won't let it happen to my lamb," Lynne insisted as she stared defiantly into the eyes of her father.

Their father looked at his daughter and son and shook his head in resignation. "I'll tell you what we'll do. Rich, your lamb will be sold because . . ."

"That's not fair, Dad," Rich sputtered.

"Hear me out, Rich. Yours will be sold because he's a breeder and you'll still be able to see him so he won't really be gone. Also, you can keep the money that he brings in at auction."

Lynne watched her brother as he thought about their father's suggestion and finally, because he had not an ounce of maternal instinct he agreed, trying to hide his smile at the thought of the money jingling in his pocket.

"Now Lynne. I will allow you to keep your lamb. This once," he said as he held up his finger and looked sternly into his daughter's tear-stained face. "If you decide to get another lamb next year, I will not repeat this. Animals have to pay their way on a working farm. A sheep only has value as meat, as a breeder or for their wool. They are not guests. Perhaps, with luck, your lamb will produce good wool and you can learn to weave. It is only this time, Lynne," he said and then smiled as his daughter, with a squeal of happiness, flew into his arms.

# THE DILEMMA

J ANET WAS BORN in the short time when night was still hovering and morning had yet to smile upon the day when her mother, with a final effort, pushed her only daughter into the world.

From those early minutes of life, Janet was determined. With a feisty nature, she was often told that she was not the easiest of her mother's four children to raise. Having strong opinions, with an equally strong sense of persistence, mischief became her constant companion.

Times were hard then for those living in the northern interior, with little money, many miles to go for supplies and long, cold winters. But neighbors were good and community spirit was strong.

At two, she often wandered across open fields to the neighbor's house half a mile away. And when home rules became oppressive, she took up residence in the dog's house. 'Where is she?' was often the question asked and, 'What is she up to now?' followed shortly thereafter.

When Janet was older, her parents often read her the story about the obstinate little girl in hopes of showing her the problems stubborn little girls can find themselves in when they don't listen to their parents. With four active children, her hardworking parents were convinced she was sent to earth to make their lives more difficult.

With only a short, unpleasant period of time when they had lived in town next door to her mother's parents, the family again moved back to their country way of life. Instead of the sounds of traffic, they once again heard the songs of birds, the rustling of leaves and moos from neighboring cows. With a house waiting to be completed, piles of stumps to be burned as they cleared land, and animals to be tended, the children played largely unsupervised on their ten acre playground. They built forts out of ferns and played in the hollowed-out stumps of huge long-ago logged trees.

At very young ages, they were completely comfortable with the forest and neither their parents nor they were fearful of their explorations even as they traversed further and further afield.

Janet and her brothers learned many lessons by growing up in the country; animals were their playmates and the forest a second home. As they grew older, they were allowed to go fishing, eventually learning to catch their own trout that their mother cooked for dinner. They hiked up the mountain following well worn animal trails and discovered old mining equipment in creek beds as well as musty smelling miners' shacks. Janet's brothers fortunately had an unerring sense of direction. As they grew older, they were allowed to take their bikes and ride to the neighborhood lake.

When Janet became a young adult, she realized how fortunate they were to be able to explore wherever their adventures took them. They hadn't realized, as children, how lucky they were to be living in a time when it was safe to do so. They were able to enjoy the nature that surrounded them and see beauty that few young children now are able to see unless accompanied by their parents.

"There were few rules when I was a child," Janet told her friend. "We left in the morning, promised to be careful, and to be home by dinnertime. If we weren't home by dinnertime, that's when the rules came crashing down upon our heads. But this happened seldom. Our sense of timing was almost as accurate as our sense of direction."

"I didn't have many restrictions either," her friend replied. "Often I'd bike over to my friend's house and then we'd go down and spend time on the wharf talking to the fishermen. We also found an old vacant house. We called it 'Fanny's House' and it entertained us for several summers, in spite of the bats circling in the attic rooms upstairs."

"Jamie," Janet called to her young son as he headed towards the front door, "you have to stay in the back yard."

"Aw, Mom, can't I just go down to Chris' house."

"Not by yourself, you're not. Why don't you phone and see if he can come over here to play?" Janet watched her son, his small shoulders slumped, walk to the telephone.

"Yes, life was great then. For my brothers and myself, our lives were not filled with a lot of 'have-to's'. Those we had consisted of doing a few chores, homework, keeping our rooms somewhat tidy and minding our manners," Janet said.

"Mom," Jamie said as he wondered into the room, "Chris isn't allowed but he asked if I could come over and play now and then stay overnight. Why can't I walk that far by myself? P-l-e-a-s-e?"

"Karel and I will go out on the sidewalk and watch you from there while you go to Chris'. But you'll have to be back by 5:00 for dinner because you have a soccer practice tonight."

"Mom, I don't want to go to soccer tonight. Chris wants me to stay at his house."

"I'll have to talk to his mother, Jamie. Maybe we can arrange it for another night instead. You still have your soccer practice. Are you ready to go now?" Janet asked as she held her hand out to her son."

"I know what you mean," Karel said as they left the house. "We had pretty good lives too. Our evenings were not filled with soccer, baseball, karate or anything else. I did have a few music lessons now and again and some swimming lessons but that was all. And we sat over dinner talking and sometimes giggling. Although giggling was not really allowed. Even as an adult, I don't see the logic of that particular rule but there were few, so I didn't make an issue of it," Karel smiled as she shook her head. "It's hard to believe that things have changed so much."

Janet leaned down to kiss her son. "I'll phone before I come to pick you up, Jamie." She watched him knock on the door before continuing. "There definitely seemed to be more time for family when we were young. Now it seems we're so busy rushing here and there, we never have enough time to enjoy our families," she said as they entered the house. "Oh, Sarah's waking up. I'll just be a minute, Karel," Janet said as she hurried up the stairs.

Karel looked around at her friend's to-die-for kitchen. They seldom had time to get together either what with all the things the children were involved in, working, PAC meetings and keeping up a home. Where did the nice family life go that we enjoyed as children?

"While I was changing Sarah, I thought about what you said about sitting around the dinner table and talking as a family. We did the same thing and it was almost like being friends with our parents. We had fun laughing and playing games together. When you had that closeness with your parents, I think you weren't as likely to go looking for trouble. I was always into mischief when I was very little, but never did anything major when I got older. I never wanted to disappoint my parents or do anything that would make them really angry with me because, well, it felt like we were friends," Janet said with a smile at her best friend.

"While we were chatting with our parents, in my family, we learned about their lives before we were born and about our grandparents' lives too. There was a lot of laughing and reminiscing about things we had done in the early days of our childhood too. We knew about family because there was time to talk about it. I don't have time to do that with my own children," Karel said. "Half the time we don't even eat dinner together because one or the other of us has to rush out to something. With Richard working on his Ph.D, he's at classes or working on projects several evenings a week. The children are all in a couple of activities each week, and with my own job . . . well, there just doesn't seem to be time to spend together as a family."

"We don't either. I always thought that part of the reason for my idyllic lifestyle, as a child, was that we lived in the boonies. We were forced to improvise and be creative," Janet said with a dreamy look in her eyes. "I'd love to have that kind of life for my children."

"I didn't live in the boonies but my life was almost as simple and carefree as yours was. Times were different and people had different expectations. People want more now. Most mothers stayed home then and families didn't have the newest and the best of everything. Look at how much our children have. Do they need it all? Nobody outgrows or wears anything out anymore because they have so much. Do they even want it all? We have toys from one end of the house to the other, and half of them are ignored," Karel said as she held out her arms for Sarah.

"I'd rather stay home and look after my children, at least until they go to school instead of having two new cars sitting in the garage. An older one would be just fine for me." Janet smiled and then lowered her voice. "But Frank likes to keep up with the Joneses and that means two incomes, this big house and all the appearances of success. Last Christmas the children got tired of opening presents, there were so many. That's decadence, as far as I'm concerned."

"I agree. And we're letting someone else raise our children, with their values, while we give them more than they need. Are we crazy?" Karel asked with a slight laugh.

"Janet?" Frank yelled from the games room. "Have you seen my Ipod Touch? Did Jamie take it?"

Janet shook her head, her blonde hair swinging with the motion. "I don't know where it is, Frank. I can't keep track of everything," she called. "I get so mad. I know he works hard. He's hoping to get that promotion but, around here, he does nothing. Yet he expects me to work full-time as well as look after the children, the house and the yard, and, keep track of things he misplaces."

"Life is certainly a lot more stressful than it was when we were kids," Karel smiled. "Richard does the same thing, especially since he went back to school."

"It would be nice if life was simpler and we weren't always striving for more and better. I remember one summer when I was young and the weather had been extremely hot, my brothers and I begged to be able to have a swimming pool in our yard. My father said we couldn't afford it but we nagged anyway. Finally he relented and said if we dug the pool ourselves, we could have one." Janet laughed at the memory. "We were ecstatic, that is until he handed each of us a shovel and we had dug for half an hour."

"Then what happened?"

"That was the end of our desire for a pool. My father was a pretty smart man because he never heard another word about having a pool. Frank would never go for a strategy like that. He'd get totally bent out of shape about the kids digging in his manicured lawn. He'd rather just yell at them."

"Do you think all our possessions and having more money than what we grew up with makes up for what we're missing now?" Karel asked.

"Oh Frank, did you find your IPod?" Janet asked as her husband wandered into the kitchen. Putting Sarah into her highchair, she fastened a bib around her neck.

"No, I didn't. What do you think we're missing," Frank stared at Karel, a frown settling on his brow. Karel was not his favorite person. He felt that Richard deserved someone who was a bit more flashy, not someone who rarely wore makeup, wore frayed jeans and who usually pulled her hair into a careless ponytail. In Frank's opinion, Karel didn't look like the wife of a professional.

"We were just talking about how much simpler life was when we were growing up when no one was trying to make bonus points in the neighborhood because everyone was in the same situation. And when families had more time to spend together," Janet said as she spooned pureed vegetables into the baby's open mouth.

"I still don't get what you're missing. Those weren't better times when everyone was struggling, wearing hand-me-down clothes and no one could afford to put their kids in hockey, dance or singing lessons. And we had to live in an old house and drive a rattle-trap car. Who would want those times back again?"

"But Frank, there was more time for family. That's what we're missing now. When I go back to work after maternity leave, I'll hardly see Sarah. I'll miss all her firsts. I probably won't see her take her first steps or say her first word. I'll pick her up in time to feed her and put her to bed. It was the same with Jamie. We may as well not have had children for the amount of time we actually get to spend with them."

"Well, Janet I have to go, I'll talk to you later." Karel leaned forward to hug her friend and saw tears filling her eyes.

Frank watched Karel leave before he turned to his wife. "Every time that woman is here, there are problems. She always get you stirred up about something."

Janet turned her back on her husband and continued to feed the baby. She'd been thinking about not wanting to put Sarah into day care for awhile. She'd hated doing it when Jamie was a baby too. Why leave her care to someone else? Daycare took almost half of her take-home pay anyway. But Frank liked the idea of his wife working because everyone he knew had a wife who worked. Frank never was good at being different—he'd never be a trend-setter.

"Are you ignoring me, Janet?"

Looking at her husband, she realized how angry he had become. "No, I'm not, Frank. We've had this discussion before about me going back to work but I've been thinking a lot about it lately. Besides you being able to claim me as a dependent, I could take a child in and do daycare. That would make up the extra money. We could cut back too in a lot of ways."

"No," Frank roared. "I don't want to come home after a tiring day at work and trip over toys. I absolutely won't agree to your idea, Janet."

Janet watched his retreating back as he stormed from the room. 'You're not the only one who has something to say about it, Frank,' she thought as she finished feeding Sarah. Glancing at the clock on the stove, she realized that it was almost four o'clock. She'd have to get dinner started so that it was ready by five when Frank liked it. And Jamie's soccer practice started at six-thirty. But he wanted to stay at

Chris' overnight. 'Well, why not?' she thought suddenly. Their life was always so rigid. It was Spring Break, why not try some flexibility for a change?

Lifting Sarah out of her highchair, she lay her on her mat with some toys and then got the potatoes. "Hello, Ellie," Janet said when she called Chris' mother, "how are the boys doing? Oh, thank you, that's always nice to hear. Yes, Jamie mentioned that he'd been invited to stay overnight. Are you sure that's not too much trouble? I know he'd love to stay. I'll bring his toothbrush and pyjamas over later." She smiled to herself as she put the potatoes into boiling water.

As she prepared dinner she continued to remember periods from her life as a child. One particular time that always brought pleasant memories was when she and each of her brothers had been allowed to have a rabbit. Although the rabbits were supposed to stay in their cages or only come out one at a time, neither of the children could see the logic in that. After many such visits, their father was soon building more rabbit cages to pen the growing rabbit population.

"We'll have to sell some of them. We can't keep them all," her father had told them.

"That isn't fair," Janet bravely announced, "they're our rabbits."

"And can you afford to feed them all, young lady? And what about looking after them? Who's going to do that?"

"We will," they'd all chorused together.

"And we'll pay for their food out of our allowance," Janet said.

Looking at each of his children, her father had finally relented. "But," he said as he held up his finger to prove the seriousness of his statement, "there is no letting them all out together anymore."

"Why?" Janet's youngest brother had asked.

Looking at each of his children, he finally shook his head and said, "Because if they play together, they will just keep having more baby rabbits."

Janet remembered that that statement had stopped them in their tracks. "You get babies from playing together?" they wondered.

She remembered her parents' laughter when she had finally decided to ask her mother if she should stop playing with other children.

As Janet watched Sarah trying to pull her sock off her chubby foot, gurgling to herself as she tried, she thought, 'With two parents working, my children will never be able to experience the kind of fun and commitment there was in being responsible for your own animal.' Janet smiled as Sarah finally gave up and rolling onto her side, picked up the fluffy teddy that had been her favorite toy almost from birth.

Janet got a fresh diaper and knelt on the floor to change Sarah. "Hi Baby, you're such a good little girl." Her heart expanded within her chest as she smiled at her daughter. 'How could she put this baby into daycare?' she thought.

"Is dinner ready?" Frank called from the living room where he was plunked in front of the television, his laptop on the coffee table in front of him.

"Almost," she answered as she washed her hands at the kitchen sink. Draining the potatoes, she got the butter and milk out of the fridge.

Her mind drifted back again to her childhood. It had been a good childhood and she wanted her children to have one that they would also look back on with happiness. Not one where all they could remember is being shuffled from one daycare to another and hardly seeing their parents before being hustled off to bed. She decided with determination that she was going to enjoy her children and have a real family life like she had grown up with.

"Frank, dinner is ready," Janet called. Lifting the baby and giving her a quick hug, she put her into the highchair and gave her a teething biscuit to chew on while they ate. Frank liked to eat his dinner in relative quietness.

Her husband dug into his food as if he'd forgotten he'd had two grilled cheese sandwiches, a handful of cookies and two glasses of milk for lunch. Janet eyed the plumpness of his belly as it threatened to spill over the top of his pants.

Glancing at his face, she realized he was still out of sorts from their earlier conversation. 'Well,' she thought, 'I'm not giving in this time. I did with Jamie and I've regretted it ever since. I'm not putting another baby into daycare. He gets his way in almost everything, he's not going to this time.' She smiled at her daughter, the wispy curls on her head moving slightly as she bounced and laughed happily.

"You're spoiling the kid. That's another reason why I think it's a good thing for you to go back to work. I can't stand spoiled kids," Frank muttered, bits of the bun he was eating flying out of his mouth as he spoke.

"Being an only child, do you think you were spoiled when you were growing up, Frank?"

"This isn't about me," Frank thundered.

'It's always about you, Frank,' Janet thought to herself. 'You don't want toys around, you don't want kids around, you want all the fancy things and you want to be waited on. When do you ever give? When do you spend time with your children, give them a hug or tuck them into bed?' But she said none of these things.

Janet smiled at her husband as she thoughtfully chewed the tender chicken. "What time do you have to go in to work tomorrow?"

He frowned in her direction. Janet knew he suspected she was up to something. 'I'm not yet, my dear, but I'm certainly thinking about it,' she thought. "Too bad you couldn't take some time off during Spring Break. It would be a good chance to spend some time with the children."

"I'll take some time off when it's quieter; it would be more of a rest for me then." He got up and threw his napkin down onto his empty plate. "If there's dessert I'll have it in the living room."

Janet watched him leave the room. She knew she had a perfectly viable argument. She cleared twenty-two hundred dollars a month after taxes and deductions and they'd have to pay one thousand a month for daycare for Sarah plus the after school care for Jamie. That barely left twelve hundred dollars that she'd be earning for leaving her child. Working cost money with extra car insurance, gas and clothes too. But if she looked after one child, it would be company for Sarah and she'd probably make eight hundred to one thousand dollars depending on the age of the child. She could easily make up the difference by cutting back and taking advantage of sales, bargains and coupons. Then Frank could claim her as a dependent and they'd probably be ahead of the game. 'He has no real valid reason for me to go back to work,' she thought angrily. 'And the children would love to have me at home. I would have more time to help Jamie with his school work and I could help in his classroom.'

Wiping Sarah's hands and face, she lifted her up. "We'll get Daddy his pudding and then it's time for a cuddle and your bottle, Sweetie. And then I have to clean up the kitchen."

Janet sat in the recliner chair and watched Sarah's face as she drank her night time bottle. The baby's eyes never left her own until slowly her eyelids drooped and finally closed, her grip on the nipple lessening as she drifted off to sleep. After tucking her into her crib, Janet gathered up Jamie's overnight things in readiness for taking them over to Chris'.

"I'm going to run these over for Jamie, he's staying overnight. Sarah is asleep but I won't be long."

"These kids have it so soft. Why doesn't he come and get them himself?"

"He could and would if I didn't worry about him being on the street by himself. Life is much different than it was when we were growing up, Frank. Things were safer then," Janet said.

"I think you're making a mistake, you're making a sissy out of him. Boys have to grow up to be tough."

"Frank, I'm not going to argue with you. There are things regarding parenting that we don't agree on and probably never will but since I'm the one who is doing most of the parenting, I'm going to do it the way I feel keeps our children the healthiest, happiest and safest."

"Are you saying I'm not a good parent?"

"I didn't say that. I'm saying that we disagree so why don't we just agree to disagree and drop the whole subject. All this arguing never gets us anywhere."

Janet watched as Frank threw up his arms in exasperation and walked angrily back into the living room. Shrugging, Janet put Jamie's sleepover things into his backpack and quietly closed the door behind her.

"Hi Ellie," she smiled, "it doesn't sound like there's two little boys here," Janet said as she greeted her neighbor.

"They're busy playing with the new Wii game Chris just got."

"Did we miss his birthday?"

"Oh no, Janet. He wanted it and it's a long time until his birthday so we decided to get it for him. It's not like we can't afford it so there's no reason to wait." Ellie smiled with the hint of an embarrassed shrug.

"Karel and I were just talking about how much our children have. And we were discussing about whether they really need it all. In spite of all they have, they're more bored than we ever were as children. How do you feel about it, Ellie?"

"I know what you're saying, Janet. But my parents struggled and we didn't have much so it's nice to be able to get whatever we want and not have to wait."

"We've become an instant gratification society. When we don't have to work towards something, do we really appreciate it as much, do you think?"

"I know you, Janet. You've got some idea buzzing around there inside your head. What are you planning?"

"Well, I've been thinking lately that I don't want to put Sarah into daycare. I want to stay home and look after her myself, at least until she's a little bit older."

"I don't blame you. Kurt and I have talked about it and if we have another child, I'll do that too. He's in total agreement with it. He said it was different when Chris was born because he had just got his degree and we were so broke. But now we've got what we need and anything else is just a bonus."

"I wish Frank felt the same way. He is completely against the idea of me not going back to work. We've been arguing about it for weeks."

"I have an idea," Ellie smiled. "Kurt and Frank have a golf game planned. I'll put a bug in Kurt's ear and maybe he can put a guy spin on the idea. It can't hurt."

"I would appreciate any kind of help I can get to turn Frank's thinking around."

"Karel, you'll never believe this! It's settled, I'm not going back to work, at least not for a while. I'm going to stay home and look after Sarah myself."

"How did you manage that? I didn't think Frank would ever relent."

"Kurt and Frank went golfing and Kurt gave my theory the male approach. You know what they say, Women are from Venus and Men are from Mars, well it's true. We don't talk the same language or even think alike. It's all a matter of presentation apparently."

"What did Kurt say to Frank?"

"I don't know; he wouldn't tell me. He said I wouldn't understand because I'm from a different planet. I wasn't sure how to take that but decided it was in my best interests to keep my mouth shut."

"I think that was a very wise decision."

# A FAMILY MATTER

IS DARK HAIR, now showing streaks of gray, swung low on his forehead. His face grew crimson as his anger increased. Maggie could see the blue veins as they bulged in his temple and the muscles in his jaw as they twitched uncontrollably. He clenched his fists, the bones of his knuckles white splotches against the tan of his skin.

He glared angrily at the wood as if the fault was in the wood rather than anything of his own doing. Maggie could see that each piece was numbered but he ignored these basic instructions as he struggled to put the jigsaw pieces together. The cabinet had been his idea. Although Maggie and her mother were not happy that his guns would be so accessible to him, neither had dared voice any opposition to it.

She watched quietly. From past experiences, when he was in a mood such as this, she knew it was best to stay out of his line of vision. To get up and walk out of the room would have drawn attention to her presence. She and her mother tried to fly below the radar screen when he was in a foul mood. Maggie suspected that may not be possible this time as she watched his anger escalate.

Muttering angrily beneath his breath, he'd finally bellowed in a voice like a disgruntled bull. "Karen, where is the rest of the wood?" Spittle flew from his mouth with each word he uttered.

Maggie's mother, nervously drying her hands on a worn towel, looked hesitantly into the living room. "There wasn't anything else, Kevin. You brought it in yourself."

Her mother's voice, timid as usual, irritated Maggie. *'Why does she let him do that to her?'* she wondered as she had so often over the years. *'I hate him!'*

"Where is the other box?" His voice had become harsh and brittle as his anger consumed him, like crackling flames racing across a dry prairie landscape.

"There wasn't another box, Kevin," Karen said. Her voice was barely above a whisper, a sharp contrast to her husband's frightening sounds.

Maggie wanted to take her mother's hand and leave. She knew her father's temper would only get worse. When Maggie looked at her mother's thin face, she saw the fear, and the slight trembling of her bony shoulders. Shifting in her chair, her father's head swung angrily in her direction. Each stayed to protect the other but she never had been able to protect her mother and her mother had been unable to protect herself.

"You're lying to me." Maggie watched him struggle drunkenly to his feet. "*Run,*" she urged her mother desperately. "*I'll look after myself.*" But she knew her mother wouldn't think a girl of only twelve would be able to look after herself.

Unable to stand the thought of what she knew was going to happen next, Maggie got up and walking in a wide half-circle around her father, she grasped her mother's hand. "Mom, let's leave," she said as she tried to pull her mother along with her.

"Get out of the house, Maggie," her mother whispered urgently. Her voice, thin and high with fear, was unlike her familiar sweet voice. "Go to the Wilson's."

Her father paid no attention to his daughter; his eyes were riveted on his wife's face. Her mother stared back at him with a defiant expression on her pale face. Maggie had never seen that look of determination on her mother's face before. It made her more frightened than ever before.

"Go, Maggie," her mother whispered insistently.

As Maggie lay in bed, she thought back to that terrible day eight years ago. It was the day her whole life had changed. She'd lost her father, which, when she thought about it, was no great loss. But she had lost her mother too. That had been the greatest loss of all.

Maggie had not been allowed to see her mother. It had seemed like years but in actual fact it had only been a few months before they led Maggie into that bleak, gray, cold room. Her mother had looked even smaller than she had before things had gone so dreadfully wrong. She'd tried to smile at Maggie but her mouth had quivered uncontrollably and tears had cascaded desperately down her sunken cheeks. She'd covered her mouth in an attempt to still her trembling lips but had not been successful.

"Mom, why have they done this to you? It's not fair. He did awful things to you, to both of us." Maggie looked at her own trembling hands clenched tightly in her lap, tears streaming down her own face. Then raising her head, she'd said, "I think he deserved to die, Mom. I'll tell them all the awful things he's done to you, to us. I'll tell them about your broken arm and your broken jaw, about your black eyes, and how many teeth you've lost because of him. The way he treated us must matter."

Maggie watched as her mother tried to speak but she had been unable to form the words. The guards had finally come and taken her mother back to her dark, lonely cell.

Maggie had gone to live with her aunt and uncle; her only blood relatives. He was her father's only sibling. During those years, her uncle had tried to poison her young mind against her mother but she could never forget the cruel things her father had done. Uncle Todd had never been able to turn her against her mother.

Tossing and turning, Maggie spent little time in sleep. Her mind, like a movie screen, kept replaying pictures of the few times she had seen her mother. She glanced at the clock repeatedly but the minutes ticked slowly by while she waited for morning. Tomorrow her mother was going to be returned to her.

"Mom," Maggie yelled when she saw the small, thin woman walk through the heavy metal gates. "Oh Mom, things are going to be good for you now. I'm going to look after you." The words tumbled from her lips while tears streamed down her face.

Her mother smiled, tears filling the shallow pools of her eyes also. "I don't expect you to look after me, dear. I plan on getting a job." She looked around uncertainly. "Somewhere," she added vaguely but her voice no longer sounded timid.

Maggie had seen her mother periodically in the first few years before her uncle's family had moved and she'd been unable to visit. Her uncle had forbidden her to make the two hour trip on her own and her aunt did nothing that would anger her husband.

"But I want to look after you," Maggie smiled. "I've been waiting so long and I've missed you so much. We don't have to be afraid anymore."

As they got into Maggie's car, she studied her mother. She was smaller; or maybe it was that she herself was bigger. She didn't have the frightened look etched onto her face that Maggie was familiar with. She looked older than she remembered but, she reminded herself, so did she. Maggie suddenly realized that she no longer knew her mother.

The silence stretched as the tires of her car ate up the miles until her mother finally said, "How are you, dear?"

The words were not coming as easily as Maggie had thought they would. There had been years of nights when she had lay awake thinking about what she would like to tell her mother; imagining what she'd say in return and now neither seemed to be able to find the words they needed. They were like strangers to each other.

"I'm fine. How are you, Mom?"

*'Why am I talking like this?'* she wondered. *'I just want to hold my mother's hand and lay my head on her lap; I want to be her little girl again. Oh, I need you, Mom.'*

"Things will be different than they used to be, Maggie. I hope you'll understand that. I've changed and you've grown up. It will take time to make up for what we've lost, and to adjust. We've lost almost half your lifetime." She smiled gently at Maggie.

Maggie felt tears fill her eyes. "I've made your favorite things for dinner, Mom." She tried to smile but the lump in her throat was making it difficult."

"We could go to a restaurant but this is probably for the best. It would have seemed strange to be around people. I'd feel as if they all knew where I came from. I think I'll feel for awhile as if I have a brand on my forehead."

Silence filled the car again; Maggie felt more alone than she had for a long time. She tried to think of words but there was an empty void where her thoughts should have been.

"Do you understand what happened that day, Maggie?" her mother finally asked.

Her voice was strong and Maggie knew that the timid woman she had known as her mother no longer existed. Maggie sensed that this new woman would never again allow herself to be mistreated.

"I think so. I know he beat you terribly at times." She had known that her mother had used foundation in an attempt to cover the bruises from her daughter but Maggie had still been able to see the discoloration beneath the carefully applied make-up.

"As you grew older, his anger was sometimes directed at you. I hated what he did to me but my greatest fear was for you. On the day it happened, I had no thought other than to defend myself when he came at me with the hammer. I was not going to allow him to kill me and let him look after you without my protection. He would have treated you as he did me. I could not allow that so I had to defend myself. I had to make sure that I was not going to die."

As she remembered her mother's frightened face on that fateful day, Maggie could feel perspiration begin to coat her upper lip as the images intruded upon her mind.

"You don't have to talk about it now, Mom."

"I think it's important that you understand, Maggie. I'm not a cold-blooded murderer as your uncle tried to make believe. Your father died while I was defending myself."

"Why didn't you let me testify about how he had treated you?"

"I didn't want to put you through that—you were a child."

Maggie turned to smile at her mother. "Well, you're home now and I'm happy."

"Did they treat you well? I worried so much but there had been no one else. My only hope was that your aunt would be able to protect you."

Maggie thought about the years she'd spent with her aunt and uncle. She'd seen similar bruises on her aunt's arms and face that she had seen on her mother's but her aunt hadn't been as timid. They had often consoled each other through their difficulties.

"It was okay," Maggie answered vaguely.

"I prayed every night that you were being treated well." Her voice trailed off as she looked out at the passing landscape.

"We don't need to talk about that right now. We have to catch up on so much."

Her mother smiled sadly. "You're right, dear. You said you were having my favorite things for dinner but I have to confess I don't even remember what they were."

With a smile Maggie said, "It's a surprise. So many things will be a surprise for you."

"Aunt Hilary, we're back," Maggie called as they went through the front door.

"Karen, it is so good to have you here with us." Aunt Hilary hugged her sister-in-law tightly. "Maggie and I have been looking forward to this day for a very long time."

Maggie watched her aunt. Aunt Hilary had come a long way in the last six months. Her skin glowed; it was no longer bruised; there were smiles and laughter always on her face. Maggie hoped she would soon see this transformation in her mother's face too.

Maggie was aware of her mother's curious glances but she said nothing. 'But of course,' Maggie realized, 'she didn't know that I was still living with Aunt Hilary. She must be full of questions but the answers will all come in good time,' she thought.

"Karen," Aunt Hilary said as she looped her arm through her sister-in-law's arm. "I hope you still like everything we made you. You'll have to eat three desserts every day to get some meat on those bones though."

The table was set as it usually was with three place settings. "You've sat at this table for the last six months, Karen." Aunt Hilary smiled. "We've talked to you and hoped you'd heard us. Come, sit down. We have so many things to tell you."

Karen helped herself to the scalloped potatoes and broccoli and cheese; leaving the meat loaf. "I eat only chicken and fish now; no red meat."

Aunt Hilary laughed. "The three of us were just talking about that the other evening over dinner—about becoming semi-vegetarians. Maggie and I thought it would be much healthier. You hadn't said anything. I guess you wanted to keep it as a surprise for us."

A confused look passed over Karen's face. "Oh, I thought you were talking about Todd when you said 'the three of us'." She looked around nervously. "Where is he, by the way? I'm not sure he'd be happy that I'm having dinner here."

"It's a very long story, Karen. We'll tell you all about it once you've settled yourself in," Aunt Hilary said with a quick glance at Maggie. "We were talking last night about going on a trip to celebrate your freedom. Do you think you'd like to do that?"

"My only thoughts so far have been of getting out of prison. I still can't believe it. How does Todd feel about me being here, Hilary?"

"Don't you worry about him, Karen. We don't, do we, Maggie? We discovered if we were strong and stuck together, we didn't have to take his abuse. It's time men discovered it is not their right to abuse the women in their lives."

"Mom, Aunt Hilary and I were thinking about going boating for a couple of weeks—just the three of us. Doesn't that sound exciting? We can sleep and eat on the boat. It'll feel as if we're the only people in the whole world."

"Would Todd let you go?" Karen couldn't keep the surprise from her voice.

"Well Todd can't stop me, Karen. If you want freedom, you're going to get it. There will be just the ocean for as far as the eye can see."

<hr />

Maggie watched her mother as she laughed comfortably with Aunt Hilary. She'd put on weight since she'd been home. 'She looks happier than I ever remember seeing her,' Maggie thought. They'd gone shopping for clothes, and like a young girl, her mother had excitedly tried on each new outfit.

Maggie's mother had finally agreed that a boating trip would be a wonderful way to celebrate her new-found freedom. "You were both right. I can hardly wait."

"I'm glad you're happy, Mom. What time should we leave tomorrow, Aunt Hilary?"

"We should try to be on the boat by five a.m. I'm going down to make the last minute arrangements later and maybe get some of our bags loaded early. Then tomorrow morning it will just be a matter of loading the last minute things and leaving."

"Five a.m.," Karen groaned. "Why so early if we're making up our own rules?"

"It gets busy at the marina later in the day. It's easier to get out of the bay when there aren't other boats all trying to do the same thing. Don't worry you'll have many wonderful days to be able to sleep in for as long as you want."

"What's in that long bundle we're bringing with us? It must have taken up most of the space in your freezer. Is it fish bait? Are we going fishing too?" Karen asked.

"We're bringing along some bait just in case we decide to go fishing. Okay everyone, grab your bags, and Maggie, you can help me with this bundle."

As Maggie walked behind her aunt with the rope slung over her shoulder, the weight of it cut into her flesh. It swung against their legs as they walked towards the boat.

"Untie those ropes, Maggie," Aunt Hilary beamed as she glanced back at the empty wharf. "All those sleepyheads still in bed don't know what they're missing."

Once out of the bay, Aunt Hilary opened up the motor and headed to the open waters. "We'll go where it's deep and enjoy the quietness with no other boats around. We can have lunch out there too. Later in the day, we'll head in a little closer to shore and drop anchor. When we're sleeping it's better to be a little protected from any winds that may come up during the night."

They squinted into the bright sunshine from their perch on the flying bridge, their hair blowing in the breeze. "We'd better put on some sunscreen," Hilary reminded them. "This is what complete freedom is all about, Karen."

"Where's your hat, Maggie?" Karen asked sounding like the mother Maggie remembered from her childhood.

"I'll get it, Mom." She smiled affectionately at her mother.

About an hour out, Aunt Hilary slowed the boat and turned to her niece. "I think it's time now, Maggie." Both climbed down the ladder while Karen watched from above.

"What are you doing?" she called down to them.

"It's a peace offering to those powers that were once beyond our control," Aunt Hilary answered as she tied several twenty pound weights to the ropes that were attached to the long bundle. "It represents a long ago promise made to three special women." She turned and smiled up at Karen.

"Are you ready now, Maggie?"

"Yes," Maggie grunted as they heaved and pushed the long bundle over the side of the boat. Maggie felt no misgivings, only profound relief as she saw it sink slowly out of sight.

"We've got two beautiful weeks ahead of us," Aunt Hilary said as she started back up the ladder to the flying bridge. "Break out the champagne, Maggie. I hope you girls are ready for the adventure of your life."

Above the sound of the motor and the screaming of the seagulls, Maggie heard her mother ask Aunt Hilary, "You never did tell me what happened to Todd, Hilary."

# TURF WAR

HEAD DETECTIVE OF the Major Crime Division, Matthew Williams, stood on the sandy beach, a puzzled expression altering the contours of his normally handsome visage. Shrugging further into his light-weight jacket, he pulled the collar up as the wind and rain continued to hammer him from the east. He turned his back to the pounding elements and pulled a notebook from his inside pocket.

"What do you make of it?" he asked his new partner, Detective Tiffany Meadows. He shook his head in an attempt to hide his smile, one that lurked whenever he thought of her unlikely name. 'She'd better change it if she plans to get anywhere as a detective in the police department,' he thought.

Tiffany's blue eyes, now clouded with concern, surveyed the small crime scene, an area contained in yellow police tape. In the centre lay a left foot encased in what appeared to be a man's good quality Nike running shoe. An early morning jogger had discovered the grisly remains and had called it in. "Why just a foot, Matthew?" she said.

"You'd prefer the whole body, would you, Meadows? We're going to find where the rest of the body is and where this foot came from," Matthew Williams replied curtly.

"Well, right off the bat we know it's a man's foot. And we know he wasn't a down-and-outer because that's an expensive sneaker. Maybe he fell off a boat. And I doubt very much that he was a fisherman either so it would more likely be a yacht. Fishermen don't wear expensive shoes like that. Maybe we could start checking out boating accidents; especially since there's been such stormy weather lately. Have there been any missing persons reports lately?"

Williams glared at her. "What makes you think it was washed up and not dropped here?"

Tiffany stared back at the senior detective, refusing to be intimidated. "I know you don't think I'm very bright Matthew but you haven't given me a snowball's chance in hell of proving I can be a good detective. Every time I say something, you shoot me down." She placed her hands on her hips and stared defiantly into his face. His dark eyes bore into hers. "Just look at the shoe," she continued, "it looks waterlogged and, if you look closer, instead of trying to find fault with everything I say, you'd see that the part of the ankle that's exposed above the top of the shoe looks as if it's been in the water for some time, like we look if we stay too long in a bubble bath."

"I wouldn't know. Bubble baths aren't my thing. Are you trying to be a trouble maker here, Meadows?"

"You asked me what I made of it, so I'm telling you," Tiffany suddenly flashed Williams one of her spectacular smiles. "And also, since you did ask me, you do remember, don't you that about two months ago another left foot was washed up on the banks of the Golden River. That one had a rather unusual tattoo of a dragon curling around the ankle. Wouldn't it be interesting if this one did too?"

"You don't need to act like a know-it-all, Meadows, I'm not verging on dementia. We're still working on the origins of that foot. And yes, before you get too cocky, there quite possibly is a connection between the two left feet." Matthew didn't know why she got under his skin; most times she was a major pain in the butt but, he thought to himself, she did have a killer smile.

"Are you sure you don't have high blood pressure, Matthew? I'd have it checked out if I were you,"

Tiffany winked. "By the way . . ." Matthew's cellphone rang shrilly. Tiffany watched as he took it out of his pocket almost dropping it in the sand in the process. She suppressed a giggle.

"What? Are you sure? We'll be right there. Come on Meadows, move it. Tony," he said turning to one of the other police officers, "make sure this crime scene is not disturbed until it has been completely processed. I'll talk to you later."

Once in the car, Williams put his siren on and pulled quickly into traffic. "What's going on?" Tiffany yelled above the noise of the siren.

"A male, in his twenties was discovered in a stairwell downtown. If he hadn't been found when he was, he would've bled to death. He's been badly beaten and, get this Meadows, he's missing a foot. He's in St. Mary's Hospital."

"Which foot is it?" Tiffany for once was almost speechless.

"The right one. There are similarities but it makes the whole case even more puzzling. Any ideas?" He banged his hand on his forehead.

'Fool,' he thought. 'Why give her an opportunity to come up with any more of her lame brain theories?'

Tiffany was silent for a few minutes while she digested the new information. "Did he say anything when he was brought in?" she finally asked.

"How do I know, but hopefully I'll get some information out of him when we get there," Williams said. A smug look settled over his features.

"Well, I have a few ideas but I'm going to keep them to myself for now because you obviously don't appreciate them," Tiffany smiled. Settling back in her seat, she kept her eyes fastened on the road as Williams wove dangerously through rush hour traffic.

'Praise the Lord,' Williams thought; a silent Meadows was indeed a treat.

Rushing into the hospital Detective Williams caught the attention of an emergency room nurse as she tried to hurry past. Showing his credentials, he said, "We'd like to speak with the young male that has just been admitted. The one with the missing right foot."

"I'm sorry, I can't allow that. You'll have to wait until he's been stabilized," she said before quickly disappearing through a set of swinging doors.

"Well, I can't wait. I need to know who this person is. I'm sure there's a connection," Williams muttered to Tiffany. "You wait here, Meadows."

"Not likely, Williams, I'm coming too." Tiffany finger-brushed her windblown blonde hair back from her face as she followed her partner.

At the end of the hall, several nurses hovered around a curtained partition. Looking purposeful, the two detectives walked to the curtained area beside the huddle of medical staff. Ignoring the patient in the cubicle, they pulled the curtains around themselves. The occupant wheezing on the bed did not appear to be aware of his visitors and his laborious breathing covered any sound they made. Williams furtively looked around the dividing curtain of the cubicle. Dropping it quickly as if it was a sheet of flames, he motioned for Tiffany to follow him.

"What was that all about?" Tiffany demanded when they were out of earshot. "If we're leaving so quickly, what exactly did we accomplish by coming here?"

"Keep your voice down. I recognized him. He's Trung Pham, leader of the rival gang of Enrique Gonzales' gang. They call themselves Dua Rong, Dragon Lords. They've become more visible lately and have almost eclipsed the Hardrocks as Gonzales' main contender in the drug war."

"How did you recognize him? I thought you said he was badly beaten."

"He has a scar running from the corner of his eye to his chin. It's a red and blue dragon tattooed as if it's twisting itself around the scar. Once you've seen it, you'll never forget it."

"The same tattoo that was on the ankle of the first foot that was found?" Tiffany's voice rose above its usual soft tones. "What does that say to you, Williams?" she asked as she stood with her hands on her hips and glared at the imbecile who was her partner.

"Keep your voice down. Do you want everyone to hear? That's what we're doing Meadows, we're finding out. We're working on a case here and we don't have to tell everyone within earshot. Come on, let's get out of here." Williams continued to grumble under his breath as they walked towards the exit doors.

"What are you muttering about, Mr. Williams?"

"Why, are your ears burning?" As they walked out the door, the gusting wind and driving rain hit them with a vengeance. "Damn, I forgot about this blasted weather," Williams said. "But if my suspicions are correct, there will be more than one storm we're going to have to endure over the next few days."

"Where are we heading?" Tiffany asked as she followed Williams to his vehicle.

"You're not going anywhere, Meadows. I'm dropping you off at your car," he said as he strode quickly ahead of her, turning up his collar as he went.

Running to catch up to him, Tiffany called, "Oh no you don't, Williams. I'm stuck as tight to you as the remaining sand on your shoes. You probably didn't realize that you'd left clumps of it on the floor in the emergency room."

Williams gave her a withering look before turning the ignition in his car. "Okay, but you won't like it. We're going to pay a little visit to Gonzales. We'll see if he has any answers for us. Probably won't get much. On my last meeting with him, he behaved as if he'd done nothing more evil than what he'd been guilty of on the day he was born. Just thinking about the things he's done and what we've never been able to pin on him makes my ulcer bleed and my head want to explode with anger." They drove in silence until they turned onto a rutted gravel driveway. "Oh, oh, looks like he's got lots of company. You sure you still want to be a part of this, Meadows?"

As they got out of the car, Tiffany said, "Do you want to keep your right foot, Williams?" She stood with her legs planted solidly and her slim shoulders thrown back. He had no doubts that he was stuck with her. As he knocked on the door he glanced over at his partner and realized she was ready for anything. The door opened as far as the chain would allow and a belligerent black eye glared at them.

"What are you doing here, Williams?" Gonzales asked as he undid the chain. "Have you seen a ghost or are you just chasing them?"

Williams threw his shoulders back and did his own imitation of a tough guy. "Wanna step outside, Gonzales. We gotta talk."

"Sure Williams. I got nothing to hide." He shut the door behind him. "So, what's up, Detective?"

"There's a guy down in Emerg at St. Mary's missing his right foot; do you happen to know anything about that?"

"Heh, Williams, we're not surgeons; it's not feet that give us problems, it's mouths, big ones. If anybody ever wanted to get rid of someone, and we're not like that as I told you before, there are better ways to do it."

"Uh, this fellow in Emerg, he's got an interesting tattoo around a scar on his face, a red and blue dragon, does that help your memory any?"

Gonzales' face turned a sickly gray and beads of perspiration began to form on his upper lip. His hand trembled as he pushed his hair from his forehead.

"So what can you tell me about this, Gonzales?" Williams said.

"It's not what *you're* thinking, Williams but if it's what *I'm* thinking, there's a whole lot of trouble coming down."

"Oh my Gawd, it can't be," Tiffany's face was gray like the snow-filled clouds overhead.

"What are you doing?" Williams yelled as she waded toward the body partially submerged in the freezing water. Tiffany ignored the icy water as it crept higher up her legs.

"Didn't you know?" Tony asked Williams. "She's been dating him for months. Somebody shoulda thought before letting her come out here. Curtis was working on the mystery of the other foot; he must have got too close to something somebody didn't want him to know. You knew him better than the rest of us, except maybe her. What a crummy way to go." Tony shook his head.

"Meadows, get out of there," Williams yelled as he waded towards Tiffany where she stood in the water, shock and grief distorting her pretty face. She seemed oblivious to the wind whipping her hair or the sleet pounding her face. Grabbing her arm, he dragged her, with little resistance, out of the crashing waves. Motioning to Tony, he threw him his keys and pointed to his vehicle. "Turn the heat on, I'll be there in a few minutes."

Williams stared at the tattoo. It was like a medal pinned on Curtis' bare chest and was the same as the one on Trung Pham's face. Williams heard footsteps in the sand behind him. Turning to Tony, he said, "What do you make of the tattoo, Tony? It's a gang member's tattoo. Meadows must have known about it."

"My guess is he probably got it so he could infiltrate the gang; I knew he was working undercover. She should get out of her wet clothes," Tony said as he motioned with his head towards the car.

Gusts of wind and sleet bombarded them. "I'll drop her off—see if someone can stay with her. Then I'll head down to Emerg again and try to get some answers," Williams said as he shivered in his own sopping pants and squelching shoes. 'The joys of police work,' he thought as his cellphone rang. Answering it, he walked towards his car with a final wave at Tony.

He stopped suddenly when he saw something in the water, moving slowly back and forth with each undulating wave. It was a watch, unique in style, with an unusual brown leather wristband. Inside the band was inscribed: 'Life for life, eye for eye, foot for foot, Exodus 21:23'. He dropped it into a baggie and put it into the inside pocket of his jacket. "Yeah, we'll meet you there. She's not in too good a shape right now though." Inspector Morrison was always short on sympathy but he was probably right in this case.

When Williams climbed into the car, Tiffany was ashen and shivering, her teeth chattering even in the warmth of the car. He turned the heat up as far as it would go. "We're going to the Policeman's Club; get you something to eat and throw around some ideas. Feel up to it?" He knew if he showed her any sympathy, the tears would flow. And now was not the time for an emotional breakdown.

She shrugged, keeping her eyes averted.

"Did Curtis ever say anything to you about what he was working on?"

Her head shot up. "How long have you known?"

"I only just found out. We're going to discuss some ideas with Inspector Morrison; toss around what we know or suspect and between us we should be able to come up with some answers. I want to get whoever did this to Curtis as much as you do, Tiffany." Williams leaned over and awkwardly patted her hand, as if she were a small child.

"Eat," he told Tiffany when the clubhouse sandwich had been placed in front of her. "And get that coffee into you. We don't want you going into shock." Pulling the baggie from his pocket, he pushed it across the table toward Morrison. "I thought this was rather interesting," he said. "I found it in the water near . . ."

Tiffany's eyes grew large in her white face but she said nothing. 'She knows something,' Williams thought as he watched the kaleidoscope of emotions flash across her countenance. 'I wonder exactly how deep Curtis was in all this?'

Inspector Morrison hadn't missed the expression on Tiffany's face either. "I think you'd better tell us all you know, Detective Meadows. Your life could be in danger too. How far was Curtis into the gangs?"

Williams handed her a tissue as tears began to splash down her face. "He knew his life was possibly in danger. But he didn't say anything that indicated that what he was working on was connected to the foot that had been found. He was working with a drug gang and on something to do with a ship from Port of Chimbote in Peru. He was trying to get onto the ship. I hadn't talked to him for several days and was starting to worry that . . . that . . . something had happened to him."

"Do you happen to know the name of the ship, Detective Meadows?" Inspector Morrison smiled at her as he picked up his roast beef sandwich. "Do you think they really thought he was one of them or did Curtis suggest that they may be getting suspicious of him?"

"I think he felt fairly secure; he didn't indicate otherwise to me. The ship was the Santa Cruz." She turned to Williams, the trail of tears beginning to dry on her face. "I think he'd had some dealings with Gonzales too; it may have had something to do with the ship. But I don't think it had anything to do with the foot even though that was what he had originally started working on. Somehow he happened to find out about the huge drug deal that was taking place. He did have a notebook though. If we could find it, we might be able to find out more information."

"I know how we can get more info on the Santa Cruz. There's a longshoreman who works down on the docks, a good guy, and he may be able to fill us in on a few things." Williams took the last bite of his clubhouse and washed it down with the last dregs of his black coffee. "Finish up there Meadows, if you plan to come with me."

"Hi, Jimmy, how are you doing? We're looking for information about the Santa Cruz out of Peru; you know anything about it?"

"It was due to leave three days ago but there she sits," Jimmy answered with a sweep of his hand. "You hardly ever see anyone around either which is strange. Usually there are a lot of guys bustling around before a ship's gonna leave."

"Is she loaded now?" Williams asked as he looked at it towering above the wharf.

"Looks to be. I was off for three days but with a full load of containers it would be about 175,000 tonnes. Seems to be sitting pretty low in the water right now."

"What's she carrying?" Tiffany asked.

"I heard car parts and motorcycles but who knows. Oh, here comes Big Bill. He's the head honcho on the wharf and knows everything that goes on around here. If he doesn't, he'll know who to go to for the answers."

Big Bill towered over Detective Williams by a good four inches and his bone-crunching handshake left the detective wincing in pain.

"We have several questions we'd like to ask you," Tiffany said. "First, how long has the ship been in harbour, what is she carrying and what is the reason for the delay in their departure?"

"Hold on, Little Lady," Big Bill said.

Tiffany moved closer to the big man, the top of her head level with his collar bone. "Don't ever think about calling me Little Lady again," she said as she stared up into his face. "We ask the questions and we want the answers." She suddenly smiled disarmingly.

Williams suppressed a smirk. Even he would never call Meadows Little Lady. It wasn't worth a trip to the hospital. "I suggest you answer our questions," Williams said as he stepped forward.

"Uh, I don't know if I can answer all your questions but the ship has been in harbour for about six days. The crew was given two days shore leave. Unfortunately two of the crew members did not return. I'm not sure if that is the reason why the ship has been delayed. Our foreman of longshoremen has been working the docks for a lot of years. He talked to the Captain yesterday. He may be able to answer some of your questions. I'll try to get hold of him." Perspiration dotted his upper lip as he talked to Michael Chan on his cellphone.

"Big Bill," Tiffany flashed another smile at the nervous man, "have you had any problems on the docks lately with theft or missing containers?"

The large man nervously brushed his gray-flecked hair from his forehead. "Uh, apparently a container or two has gone missing. I spoke to our man who is supposed to track the containers after they're unloaded and put into our storage area. He thinks it may be the fault of one of the truck drivers possibly unloading them at an incorrect place. We're looking into it." He fidgeted nervously refusing to look her directly in the eyes.

"I understand there are waybills for keeping track of containers. I would think losing a container is not the easiest thing to do in a properly run business. Would you not agree, Detective Williams?

"Bill, you wanted to see me?" said a young, dark haired muscular man as he hurried towards the group.

"Michael, Detective Williams and Ms. uh, Meadows have some questions they'd like to ask you."

"It's Detective Meadows. Mr. Chan, do you have any idea why the two men have not returned to their ship?"

Michael Chan's eyes darted nervously at Big Bill as he ran his hand through his thick, black hair. "I couldn't really say, Ma'am, uh, Detective Meadows." Beads of perspiration were now thick on his forehead.

"Did either of the missing men have a tattoo, a rather unusual one?" Tiffany asked.

He glanced nervously at Big Bill again. "I think one of them may have had one on his arm; they may have been Chinese characters or something."

Tiffany glanced at Williams and winked. "Mr. Chan, do you know anything about stolen containers?"

With another nervous glance at Big Bill, Chan spun around and ran towards the container storage area disappearing down one of the rows near the far side of the huge lot. Tiffany quickly grabbed her cellphone from her belt and started calling for backup as Williams took off in pursuit of the man.

———∞———

"Matthew, I've been going through Curtis' notebooks and his journal and I've come across some interesting things," Tiffany said as she leisurely took a swallow of her coffee. "This is awful! Who made it, it tastes like recycled car oil?"

"How much recycled car oil have you drank lately, Meadows? It's probably not the coffee but the fact that you've let it get cold. Any coffee tastes crappy if it's gone cold," Williams said. "What did you find in the notebooks?"

"Those tattoos, they symbolize courage, power, pride and victory, or apparently their whacked out version of them. I know you've scanned the notebooks but I'm going to go slowly through them all again. He has mentioned the Santa Cruz several times as well as Gonzales and the Hardrocks. He mentions a guy named Richard Millet too. I think he's connected to the Hardrocks. What are you doing breathing over my shoulder, Williams? I'll let you read it again when I'm finished."

Williams sighed impatiently. "How long are you going to take?" When Tiffany ignored him he returned to his desk to work on a major sulk. Suddenly his head popped up. "I just had a thought, Meadows. That's a pretty unique tattoo. I'm going to check out the tattoo parlours to see if we can find the artist who did them. He might be able to tell us who he's been doing them for." A smug smile lit up his face.

"Uh, huh, good idea, Williams. It says here that Curtis was going to meet with Gonzales. He seems to be a pretty strong suspect as far as the drugs are concerned. It sounds like he knew who some of the others were who were involved too but he doesn't give any names. Damn! Look at this, Matthew. It's his last entry dated January 27th. It's nothing more than a scrawl, looks like it could have been written by a child. I last talked to him late on the night of the 23rd."

"There's something that's been bothering me." Williams went back to the January 24th entry and reread it. "That's it, I've got it. Get your things Meadows and bring the file." He grabbed his damp jacket from the back of the chair. "I think we're going to find ourselves some answers."

"Just hang on, I'll grab the phone." Tiffany slowly turned to look at Williams. "Where? We'll be right there." Banging the telephone into the receiver, she ran passed Matthew. "What are you waiting for, Williams, we've got another foot washed up on the beach over at Centennial."

"A right or a left?" Matthew asked as he ran along beside her.

"A right and oh, the guy in Emerg died an hour ago. He never did talk."

The crime scene was already cordoned off with yellow tape by the time they arrived at the site. The foot, encased in its shoe, lay where it had been deposited by the angry waves.

"Three feet, two left and a right! Where are they all coming from? This is the strangest thing I've ever seen in all my years on the police force," Tony said as he greeted the two detectives.

"Another man's foot, I would think," Williams said, "and an expensive shoe, wouldn't you say, Meadows?" He turned to her, a smile tugging at the corner of his mouth.

"I'm sure you're right, Matthew. Did you check to see if there had been any boating accidents? Also, a plane went down near one of those small islands a few months ago; perhaps we should check to see who the passengers on the flight were and if their bodies had been recovered."

"You're on the wrong track, Meadows. The last two had the same tattoos on the ankles; it's more than a plane going down or a boating accident. It has something to do with the drug trade. Don't forget Curtis' notes and I'm sure it's tied up with the Santa Cruz and Gonzales. Curtis alluded to the fact that he suspected some of the missing containers had ended up in one of the empty barns on Gonzales' property. I'm going to check that out."

"Yeah, in Curtis' notes, he said Gonzales' has got container trucks that are busy—mostly at night. Curtis suspected that Gonzales was involved with the drugs but didn't seem to think he had anything to do with the severed foot. Curtis thought someone was trying to set Gonzales up," Tiffany said. "Or maybe its the Hardrocks who want to put Gonzales' gang out of business so they can run a bigger turf. Or it could be the Dua Rong gang?"

"It's not the Dua Rong gang; the foot and the guy in the hospital had their gang tattoos. My money is on the Hardrocks. Whoever knocked off Curtis is probably trying to send the cops a serious message to back off too. They probably thought he was getting too close to finding out what was going on," Williams said.

Williams answered his cellphone on the second ring. "We're on our way, Inspector Morrison." Turning to Tony, "We'll have to leave you, Buddy. Morrison has a lead on the Santa Cruz and wants us to head over there and check it out. They've already got a search warrant and someone will meet us at the docks with it."

Jimmy Fraser saw them approaching. "I'm not surprised to see you two back here again. There were some funny goings on between the Santa Cruz and shore late last night. I saw a motor boat tied up beside it a couple of times—thought they were lowering something heavy into it. It looked suspicious so I decided to call Inspector Morrison."

"You did the right thing, Jimmy. How can we get on to the ship? We've got a warrant," Williams smiled at the older man.

As they started to follow Jimmy, Williams phone rang again. Flipping it open he heard Morrison's excited voice. "Two men, looks like they might be South American, have been found in a shallow grave out by Moody Park. Both have had their left foot removed. They'll do some DNA testing to see if the severed feet belong to the two bodies. We suspect the cause of death may have been from loss of blood but we'll have to wait for the autopsy before we know that for sure. Find out what you can about the two men missing from the Santa Cruz, Williams and hopefully we can get identifications on these two soon."

"Now we've got bodies, Meadows. Let's hear what this Captain Cubrero has to say."

"I don't think we're going to get too much out of him. He doesn't exactly look like a 'glad you're here welcoming committee'," Tiffany smiled.

"Get off my ship," Captain Cubrero said in heavily accented English. "You got no business on board."

"Afraid we do, we have a warrant," Williams waved the paper in front of the Captain's scowling face. "We have permission to search your ship from top to bottom, Sir."

Uttering an oath that neither understood, he turned on his heels and left them standing on the deck of what seemed to be an unusually silent ship.

"Nice friendly fellow," Tiffany said as she watched the man's retreating back.

"Yeah, but I'm not worried about him. Let's begin with the crew's quarters," Williams said as he started to move towards the cabins on the lower deck.

The eerie silence followed them as they went from cabin to cabin. The small cubicles told them little until they reached one where a man lay delirious, burning up with a fever. Covered by damp sheets only, he was oblivious to their presence. Pulling back the sheet, Tiffany gasped.

The stump of the sailor's left leg was covered with a dirty bandage and caked with dried blood. It was obvious the bandage had been on for a long time. The sweetish smell of gangrene floated in the air around them. "Williams, we'd better phone Inspector Morrison. This man has to get to the hospital as soon as possible. He'll die if something isn't done quickly. In fact, he'll be lucky if he makes it anyway." Tiffany's eyes were bright with unshed tears.

"I'll call Morrison. You stay here while I check the rest of the cabins. God, I hope we don't find any more of them with missing feet."

"There were the two men in those shallow graves, the one in Emerg and now this one so I think what we're going to be finding is more feet washing up on our beaches. What happened to the idea of good old-fashioned driftwood," Tiffany shook her head in disbelief. "This is the weirdest thing I've ever heard of, Matthew."

"You got that right . . ." Williams paused and with a slight smile added, "Little Lady". Tiffany's head shot up with a look on her face he found difficult to read. The air crackled between them and then she offered one of her killer smiles.

"You've used up your one and only time you get to say that. If you say it again, you'll wish you hadn't. I just appear to look easy-going but don't test me, Williams."

In an effort to regain ground he may have lost, he pulled himself up to his full height. "I'm going to talk to the Captain too. He has to know what's going on. Call me if Morrison gets here before I'm back."

Williams heard her grumbled agreement as he quickly left the small room.

As he wandered from cabin to cabin, he found little else until he reached one where the odour permeating it was similar to where the injured man lay. Bloodied sheets lay in a crumbled heap on the cot. 'Time to find the Captain and get some answers,' Williams thought as he went in search of the officer's quarters.

The Captain glowered when he saw Detective Williams approaching. His shaggy, gray eyebrows hovered over dangerously squinted black eyes and his unkempt moustache almost concealed the thin line of his angry mouth.

"You seem to have had a problem on board your ship, Captain. Do you want to tell me about it?"

The Captain remained where he was, like a statue, stubborn resistance evident in every contour of his body. He continued to stare defiantly at the Detective.

"I suggest you tell me the whole story Captain Cubrero because we will find out. Make no mistake about that. And it will be worse for you if you don't cooperate now." Williams' cellphone rang.

"Inspector Morrison, here. Another break. We got a search warrant for Gonzales' barns and found some of the missing containers from the waterfront. We're arresting him this afternoon. What have you found on the Santa Cruz?"

"I guess Gonzales isn't as squeaky clean as he was trying to convince me he was. He tried to tell me he was an upstanding, law-abiding citizen. As for the Santa Cruz," Williams glanced at the Captain who was looking decidedly more nervous, "our chief director here has decided that the cat has got his tongue. Are the paramedics on their way, our sailor boy isn't looking too healthy."

"The paramedics should be there any minute and I'm only seconds behind them. Don't let the Captain do a disappearing act on you."

"If I hear a splash, you'll be the first person I'll call. At least we're getting a few more pieces of the pie. We just need that last morsel to tie it all together. See you when you get here." Williams slowly closed his phone and putting it in his pocket, he turned to the Captain.

"Feel like cooperating now?" Williams smiled. The Captain mopped frantically at his perspiring face. "I guess we'll have to take you downtown." Hearing noises outside, Matthew glanced out and saw two paramedics board the ship with Inspector Morrison right behind them.

Taking hold of the Captain's arm, he dragged him along as he led the paramedics to the small cabin. "He's not in good shape. We haven't been able to find out how long he's been here. How's he doing, Meadows?"

She looked a little green around the gills as she shrugged. "There hasn't been much I could do. I . . . ah, need some fresh air," she said as she staggered out the door.

Williams watched her leave, a look of concern on his face before he turned to Inspector Morrison. "How's the sailor doing? Have they said?" he asked as he nodded at the man on the bed.

"They don't sound very optimistic. His vital stats aren't good. They're just getting him prepped to take to Emerg. Did you get anything out of this guy?" Morrison gave glare for glare to the Captain.

"Not a thing so far. He looked nervous when I was questioning him but it didn't force his lips to move," Williams looked with disgust at the Captain.

"I'm taking him down to headquarters, they'll get him to talk. Get Meadows out of here, she looks like she's going to keel over."

"She's okay; tough when she needs to be," Williams said as he defended his partner. 'She wasn't bad for a woman,' he reluctantly had to admit to himself although he'd never tell her that.

"Come on, Meadows, we're going to find out who Richard Millet is. I have a few theories myself. As for the containers, they caught Gonzales red-handed, he'd better get himself a damn good lawyer."

As they walked towards the car, Williams' phone rang. "Yeah?" he barked. Tiffany felt some sympathy for the person on the other end.

"I'm not surprised. I suspected something like this. Yeah, we're on our way over." Williams glanced to where Tiffany stood waiting. Her colour had returned he noticed as she stared off in the distance, her thoughts obviously elsewhere.

"Another foot Meadows, a right, on Golden River, not far from where the first one was found."

"We're headed there, I surmise? I did a bit of research into the Hardrocks and Richard Millet after I read his name in Curtis' notebook. I think I know where to start looking for him. I assume that will be the next thing on our agenda," Tiffany said as she smiled at her partner.

"Uh, yeah, why didn't I think of it?"

"Well, in case you haven't already realized it Williams, you're a lucky man to have me for a partner. Just keep going with your pleasant disposition and your great sense of humour and you'll have me as your partner forever," Tiffany told him with a brilliant smile in his direction.

Williams gave a surprised chuckle. "How old are you, Meadows? You're still pretty wet behind the ears. You've got a lot to learn yet, so don't get too cocky on me."

"There's Tony," Tiffany pointed to the group of police officers gathered on the beach as she effectively ignored her partner's comments.

"Hello," Tony called to them as they walked towards the foot as it lay on the beach. "Nothing much different than the others except this shoe is not one of those expensive varieties. But it does look to be a man's shoe again."

"I see that," Williams replied as he removed his notebook and started to make notes. "Have pictures been taken already?"

"Everything's pretty much been done here," Tony replied with a wave of his hand. "You off to check out the Hardrocks?"

"What's this? Everyone a mind reader around here?" Williams said with a laugh.

"Inspector Morrison, they've got Williams. I need back-up ASAP. We're near Boulevard at 11549 Napier. How long? Okay, I'll keep watch on the front. They can't get out the back—there's no lane access, it backs up into another yard. The fence is about six feet high and there's a vicious dog in the adjoining yard."

Tiffany watched the front of the house from behind a parked car across the street. She could feel perspiration creeping its way through the roots of her hair to the back of her neck. She wiped her top lip impatiently never once removing her eyes from the small dilapidated house with the closed blinds.

When Williams had loudly knocked, after insisting she wait in the car, they had dragged him inside, slamming the door behind them. While she waited for back-up, she had listened for any noise but had heard nothing except the continuous barking of the neighbour's dog.

As she watched nervously, a van had pulled up in front of the house next door. One man got out and opened the sliding door of the van while it idled. Just then Tiffany saw Inspector Morrison pull up and park two cars down from the van. He had two men with him, each wearing dark glasses and bulky jackets. He crossed over to where she stood as two men from the suspect's house carried another man out to the waiting van. Tiffany breathed a sigh of relief when she realized that it wasn't Matthew.

"That's the house where they're holding Matthew," Tiffany told Morrison as her heart beat erratically against her rib cage. "I don't know who the man is they're carrying."

"Okay, stay where you are and keep watching the house. There's more support coming in a few minutes. He started to run across the street to where the van sat idling, his gun drawn but as he got closer, it quickly pulled into traffic. "We'll follow the van," he yelled at Tiffany as he hurried back to his own car.

In seconds the van had turned the corner, tires squealing with Inspector Morrison following closely behind. Where was Matthew? Tiffany wondered frantically. Another car pulled into the spot where Inspector Morrison had been parked. Tiffany recognized the driver of the car from the police department. Beckoning him over, she explained what had happened and he returned to the car to confer with the other two men.

Finally giving a motion that she was to remain where she was, they walked with determination towards the rundown house. Banging on the door, they shouted, "Open up, Police!" Nothing happened. It was as silent as it had previously been.

Tiffany saw a face peer from behind a curtain in the house next door. After a few minutes, the curtain dropped and the face disappeared. After several more warnings, the two officers threw their weight against the door and the noise of splintering wood pierced the air of the quiet neighbourhood. The sudden explosion of a gun shot from inside the house startled the birds in the large chestnut tree on the boulevard, then everything was silent again.

Unsure of what she should do, she remained where she was until she saw a familiar face looking out of the broken doorway. Williams motioned for her to join them.

"I was hoping you weren't going to do anything stupid and try to come in after me. You did good, Meadows," he said as he smiled at her. "Every detective likes to know he can count on his partner. There is more than one way to help, you chose the smart one."

"Matthew, are you hurt?" Tiffany asked nervously when she noticed the blood on his pant leg. "I heard a gunshot."

"It wasn't me," he pointed to a man on the floor writhing in pain as he held his leg. Blood had soaked through his pant leg and was pooling on the floor beneath him. "An ambulance has been called. He was going to shoot me when our guys burst in. Not a minute too soon, I might add. It wasn't my gun that got him, they'd taken mine. My heart got a bit of a work-out this afternoon though. I think we should start going to the gym instead, Meadows."

"Going to the gym sounds like heaven. I'll feel a whole lot better Matthew, if we've accomplished something by this whole adventure today."

"We certainly did, my dear. I'll tell you all about it when we go get ourselves something to eat. I don't know about you but I'm starving. Near death must bring out a fierce hunger in a man." Williams cellphone rang and he grabbed it. "You got them? Glad to hear it. What about the guy they carried out? Will he make it? I think we've almost got it all tied up. The last one here was injured. Joe and Mark will follow the ambulance to the hospital and keep him under guard and Frank will stay here until the lab comes to process the place. I'll talk to you later, Inspector," Williams said as he rang off. "Are you okay with that?" Williams asked the three officers.

Seated across the table from each other in a quiet corner of the Irish Inn, Tiffany's cold hands circled her mug of hot coffee. She patiently watched as Williams wolfed down a burger and fries, liberally splashed with ketchup. With another look at her turkey wrap, she decided she wasn't really hungry but then, she hadn't gone through a near-death experience.

"You're not going to eat that?" he asked as he licked his fingertips.

When she shook her head, he reached over and grabbed it before she could reconsider. "Okay, Matthew, I've waited very patiently, now I want to hear what happened in there."

Wiping his mouth on a paper napkin, he took another drink of his coffee. Tiffany quickly picked hers up before he decided to finish that as well. "Well, there were three of them—actually four. Another man was there with a missing foot, slowly bleeding to death like the others. He was the one they carried out to the van. I'm surprised they risked doing that. They should have realized that I wouldn't have come on my own, but maybe they didn't."

"Another one? There's been so many. But did you find out why they are doing it?"

"Richard Millet wasn't there but I heard his name mentioned. It's a hang-out for the Hardrocks, there's no doubt about that. They are the ones who are doing the amputations. I imagine it's for the reason I suspected—threats and intimidation—to override the Dua Rong gang. No doubt when they got powerful enough, they'd probably have started threatening the Gonzales' gang. I have a feeling Gonzales knew about it and realized it was only a matter of time for them. It's all about threats to gain power. They were serious threats though—a choice of being crippled for life or to die a slow death. Even a lot of tough guys would come around to their way of thinking when faced with a choice like that."

"Excuse me, Williams, I'm the one who suspected the Hardrocks wanted more turf for their drug wars. You're trying to take credit for my theory," Tiffany frowned at him. "And don't look at my coffee cup because you're not getting it."

Williams shrugged and continued. "There are a few loose ends to tie up, some more questioning to do and a few more arrests to make, but nothing that will change what we now know has been going on. We've pretty much solved our case, Meadows."

Williams smiled across the table at her, a smile quite different from any he had ever used with her before. Tiffany could feel the blush creep up into her face as she gazed down at his warm hand suddenly holding hers. "We make a good team, Tiffany," he smiled again. "Come on, let's go." As they walked out, he placed his arm companionably over her shoulders. It was a good feeling.

# SULLIVAN STATION

G EORGE PETERSON LOOKED through the blurred vision of his cataract eyes and was surprised; he realized he should not have been, everything in life changes. Cities grow, as people do, and nothing ever really stays the same, not even someplace as special as Sullivan Station. It was his last wish to come home. He hadn't lived in Sullivan Station since growing up on his parents' farm but because it was his first home, he'd always thought of it as such.

Home back then had been his parents' farmhouse situated on twenty acres and surrounded by a close-knit community. The Community Hall was still standing on 152$^{nd}$ Street but it had been called Johnston Road back then.

'How old must it be?' he wondered as he gazed at the old building still painted white as it had been when he was a young boy. If his memory was correct, it had been built in 1928, he thought. Where had the years gone? They'd had good times in that Hall when the whole community had gotten together. There was always singing and dancing; the women getting together to catch up on the latest gossip, men sharing a drink and a cigarette and children running around laughing and shouting and playing hide 'n' seek. They had been great times alright. Even at ninety years of age, he still felt that same familiar tug on his heart as he had every time he thought of Sullivan Station over the years.

As George looked around, he didn't see the B.C. Electric Railway, but then he hadn't expected to either. The Railway had provided their main transportation to New Westminster and Vancouver. He remembered, when he thought about it, that they had already been phasing it out when he had left in 1940. It was sad nonetheless. He and his friends had spent a lot of time 'hanging around' as the young people now called it, at the train station when it had been the hub of the community. It had been the most important part of Sullivan Station in those days because it was their connection to the rest of the world.

And on those days, when he had been able to attend the high school in Cloverdale, he had ridden the B.C. Electric Interurban to school. It had also carried the lumber and shingles from the area, and had kept his father working at the big mill in those many lean years during the awful Big Depression.

He again blinked unsuccessfully in an attempt to clear away the blurred image. He saw the rambling white house his father had built with the new additions that had been added whenever a new baby had arrived on the scene. It seemed every year there was a new baby added to the quickly growing family. He slowly gazed around and saw the clothes line with the white sheets flapping in the breeze. He raised his hand in the still, hot air. Where had the breeze come from? He hadn't noticed it earlier.

He could see his mother, busy as she always was, a short distance from the flapping sheets. She was on her knees in the garden, weeding the vegetables that she would can for much of their winter food supply. She was always so proud of her rows and rows of canned vegetables, fruit and meat on the shelves in the root cellar beneath their house. There had been bins too for holding the root vegetables of beets, carrots and parsnips. He had hated parsnips in those days and now they were too expensive to buy. The potatoes, onions and apples had been kept down there as well. They had never starved, thanks to his mother. Or his father for that matter too because he had kept the farm going so they'd always had a ready supply of milk and meat.

"Gramps, are you okay?" He heard his grandson's voice beside him, intruding on his memories. George shook his head as he returned to the present.

"Oh yes, son. I'm fine, just looking into the past. They were good days, son." He smiled a gentle smile, lost again in the ghosts of the past.

"George," his mother called to him as she got up from her knees. "Have you fed the chickens and collected the eggs yet? And don't forget your father wants you to help him with haying this afternoon so hurry home from school, dear. We may not get too many good days before the rains come." She wiped the sweat from her brow with the back of her dirt-stained hand. "I'm glad school's almost finished for the summer break. This is a good year for the crops so your father will need more help around here than usual so he can get them all in." He saw her bend over the vegetable patch again while the hot sun beat down unmercifully on her back. She reached up to push the old straw hat she always wore further back onto her head. It was stained and crumpled with use, but he never saw his mother outside without it.

He remembered the school where he had spent the early days of his education. He had hated going to Johnston Road School during those long ago years, but he no longer remembered his reasons for not wanting to go. The school, if his memory served him correctly, had been a good one as far as schools went. He had gotten along well with both the teachers and the other students but learning had never much interested him, not in his early years and not as he'd grown older either. He had always preferred to be outside. But he had met many good friends during those days at Johnston Road School; some that he had kept until one by one they had all died, leaving only him to mourn their passing.

He particularly remembered Lenny with his straw-colored hair that always stood up on top of his head no matter what he did to it and with the circus of freckles that chased themselves across his nose. Lenny, with his booming laughter that remained part of him his whole life, extinguished only on the day he died. Looking back to those long-ago years, he remembered coming back and visiting his friend in the hospital, his body ravished with cancer but with his ever-present smile and laughter filling the hospital room. He had loved Lenny.

That had been a sad trip. He remembered later sitting in the kitchen of his parents' home in Sullivan Station after Lenny died. He'd noticed for the first time his father's gray hair and his mother's lined face and the stoop of her shoulders. It was his first realization that they too were getting old.

"Dad, why don't you sell the farm and take life easier?" he felt that familiar stab in his heart when he said the words.

"George, with all of you gone, spread all over the country, what else would we do? We'd go crazy just sitting and twiddling our thumbs," his father said. "No, this is where we belong."

"Gramps, you look a little pale. Why don't you sit down for a while? It's hot and you've had a long day. You must be tired."

Shaking his head, George felt confused. That voice didn't sound like his father's. Slowly, and with difficulty, he returned to the present. "No son, I'm fine. There are a lot of memories here. I'm just trying to remember them all. I'll be fine but it's a lot of years to remember and I want to see them all."

Walking slowly with the assistance of his cane, he guessed approximately where his parents' small farm had been. All these houses! Who could ever have imagined back then that Sullivan Station would look like this in the future? Ah, there was his father. He had been a tall man of slender build, even then beginning to bald. He was wearing a hat but he could see the sweat staining the hatband and see where the moisture flowed down the sides of his gray-whiskered face.

"Oh, George, I'm glad you're here. I'm going to be needing your help. Lucas and Peter are at the other end of the field working. Looks like it may rain tomorrow so I want to get this hay in before we do the milking. We can't let it get wet; remember what happened last year."

George automatically smiled and nodded his head. He remembered that summers had always been a busy time what with his mother's garden, the extensive potato crop and the haying; with the necessity to get as many hay crops in each season as possible. It always depended on the weather and one never knew in British Columbia whether it would rain for a month or a day. Some summers it was so blistering hot, the crops died in the field for lack of water and other summers there was so much rain, the seeds floated on top of the huge pools of muddy water. He particularly remembered this year. It had been a good one.

He remembered also the excitement when his father was on the volunteer marketing co-operative that had been formed to help stabilize the prices and prevent price cutting by the larger producers. Times had been a little easier after that when they sold the milk and potatoes and even some of the extra hay, if it had been a good year.

Turning slowly in a half circle, he saw the May Day parade that took place every year. That was always an exciting event in Sullivan Station. It was a day neither he nor his brothers had to hay, work in the fields or go to school. He still had to milk the cows though but he never really minded that. He and his brothers had had to be out in the barns every morning before 6:00 a.m. to get it done before they went to school. His mother separated the milk, made butter and cottage cheese out of what they could use and sold the rest. It was his and his brothers' job to drop off the milk to some of their customers on their way to school.

While he got the stool set up, the milking pail prepared and washed each cow's udders, he had talked to them and he swore they had listened. He felt that he was almost one with the cows as he milked, telling them things that had bothered him when his parents had been too busy to listen or he imagined his friends would've laughed at, had he told them. He'd had his favorite cows. There had been Mildred. She'd had a real funny personality. Especially when she'd occasionally flick her tail while he was milking her and he'd end up with some cow manure smeared across his face. He'd often thought he could hear her laugh saying, "Ha, I got him real good this time." It seemed as though she had always looked around to make sure that she hadn't missed and then would give a 'moo' of pleasure when she saw the result. And then there was Molly, the quietest and most serious of all of them but she was no push-over either. He was convinced that she smiled at him each morning. He knew that animals weren't the dumb creatures they were made out to be.

He had moved to Whalley, the North Surrey area, in 1940 when the King George Highway opened so he'd have a shorter trip over the Pattullo Bridge which had finished being built in 1937. His job was in New Westminster. Like his brothers before him, he hadn't wanted to stay on the farm so he, and many of his friends, had found jobs in New Westminster.

He and his new wife Emily found a small place they could afford near where the Grosvenor and Ferguson Roads met the King George Highway. Later, when their children were old enough to attend school, they went to the Grosvenor Road School. He remembered the school, which at the time was fairly new. It had been built in 1940 with six rooms. Those times had been exciting and he and Emily had felt fortunate that their children didn't have to travel too far to a school. There were others whose children had long distances to travel, often in biting cold and freezing weather.

Although Whalley had been the first home for his young family, he had never really thought of it as home when he remembered Surrey. In his mind, when he was remembering home, he always travelled back again to Sullivan Station. Why had he not come back before now?

He lifted his battered old hat and mopped his forehead with his handkerchief. Yes, he remembered now. Emily and the children! There had always been so many other places to go. Exciting places when they could afford it. It was a long trip from Ontario when you were the only one who wanted to go. Where had the time gone? 'There must have been some time during all of those years when I could have come back,' he thought. 'But no, there were always important things in our lives that had taken precedence over a whim.' And that's what it had been during those many years, particularly when money was tight.

His eyes again scanned the area he had known so well in his childhood and youth, his vision blurred again with age and memories. There was his mother, her light brown curls gently brushing the tops of her shoulders as she worked. She was busy preparing dinner in the crowded kitchen, a pail of water on the counter that she had recently drawn from the well. Often in the winter, they had to take a stick to break the ice that had formed on top of the water in the well. The slop was put into another pail which was kept under the sink. It was usually the responsibility of one of the children to take the slop out. She turned around, "Lucas, please cut the potatoes up and put them in the pot with the stew meat."

"Aw mom, that's girl's work." Lucas whined.

"Well young man, I don't see any girls around here so I guess you'll have to do it. Where did you get that attitude? We're a family and we all pitch in." She glared at him, as much as she was capable of glaring. "And Peter, the slop pail needs to be emptied."

She had been right. They had been a family and they had all pitched in. And as far as he remembered, they had all enjoyed it. Sure, they had complained, but they were boys and they hadn't wanted to look like sissies. All his brothers, Lucas, Peter and Ralph, all older, and Milton and Jack, younger, had always been close. But he was the only one left now. His mother and father had been gone many years and he still felt guilty that he hadn't seen them in the few years before they died. Ontario is so far away. 'But,' he thought to himself in another rush of guilt, 'that really wasn't a good excuse. I should have tried harder.'

As a smile hovered on his lips, he looked around and saw only the past. There were his parents smiling and chatting with neighbors they rarely had time to visit except at fairs or festivals, and his brothers laughing and running along beside the May Day parade. And there was the marching band he'd always enjoyed, but he wasn't watching it. He saw himself smiling at Emily. She had been two grades below him and he had been in love with her since sixth grade. He wished Emily had come with him but she didn't have the same feelings for Sullivan Station as he had. 'How could she not?' he wondered idly. They agreed on everything else. It had been a good marriage. He had Sullivan Station to thank for Emily and for his two wonderful children.

George smiled again to himself. He knew he'd been blessed with the children and a wife that he loved as dearly now as he did when he had first married her those many years ago. He knew he was a very fortunate man.

He thought again of his parents and saw them in his memory as their eyes met across the kitchen table, a smile touching each of their lips. And there they were—his mother standing at the kitchen sink in her faded house dress and his father, his suspenders askew, laying his hand gently on her back and slowly massaging her neck before taking up the dishtowel and drying the dishes she was putting into the drying rack. George hadn't thought before about his parents' relationship but remembering them like that now he was happy for them. They'd had each other after he and his brothers had left the family nest.

Feeling the breeze on his face again, he remembered Sundays at Sullivan Station. He saw his father sitting on the porch as he puffed on his pipe. His mother sat in the rocking chair beside him knitting socks; he could hear the click of the needles and smell the smoke from his father's pipe. He had always liked that smell. He knew it was Sunday because Pop only smoked his pipe on that day. He always called it his day of rest, although it never really was; the cows always had to be milked.

"George," his father called to him as he heaved himself out of the chair. Would you come for a walk with me down to the barn? I have something I want to show you."

They had walked out to the milking barn and his father had rummaged on the old table that was used to keep extra things they needed out there so they wouldn't have to run into the house all the time.

"Oh, here it is," he said as he held up an issue of the farm catalog. "They have those fancy new milking machines advertised; it would cut milking time in less than a half. Your mother isn't convinced that we need it but then she ain't doing the milking. I'm not complaining about your mother; I'd never do that, she's a fine woman, but I find the arthritis in my knees makes milking more difficult every day. Especially in the winter time."

George remembered that he had nodded and the following Christmas he and his brothers had gotten together and bought the machine for their father. When he'd opened his gift that year, it was the first time George had seen tears slide down his father's lined face. George felt himself choke up at the memory.

Several months ago George had spoken to Emily about returning to Sullivan Station for a last visit. He had decided that this was the last thing he wished to do before he died. She had agreed that if he wanted to, that he should do it. That was exactly like his dear Emily; she never begrudged him anything. And now he was finally home!

Gazing around him, he smiled at the wonderful memories. From somewhere in the distance he heard his grandson's voice calling, "Gramps? Are you alright? Gramps . . ."

And then slowly, like a gentle mist, his grandson's voice slowly faded away . . . .

# A DAUGHTER'S GUILT

"YOU KNOW WHAT'S happening, don't you?" the social worker stared at Judy, sympathy creating two ridges between her dark eyebrows. "She's trying to make you feel guilty so that she can get her own way. It's called manipulation."

"I do feel guilty. She's my mother and she's old. I can't feel any other way, but I just can't look after her!" Large tears cascaded down Judy's thin face. She ineffectively mopped at the falling tears with a soggy tissue. "I'd be a nervous wreck in no time at all if I tried; she can be so demanding."

"When someone refuses to eat or threatens to throw themselves down the stairs in order to make their family do what they want; well, we take those types of threats seriously. Those kinds of behavior won't be allowed around here." Marion smiled to take the bite out of her harsh words.

"She would never try any of this with my brothers. Well, they'd never put up with it for one thing." Judy dabbed again at her puffy eyes.

"That's the secret Judy, they'd never put up with it. It is almost always the daughters that I end up talking to. Very rarely are the sons closely involved in the care of their elderly parents. And as such, the daughters are usually treated worse in spite of the care they give their ageing parents. It's not fair but it is a fact of life."

Judy's tears continued their relentless pilgrimage down her face. "She wants my constant attention. She doesn't realize, or seem to remember, that I have children and young grandchildren that I would like to spend some time with too. It isn't that she's not being looked after; they're very good to her where she's living. And I see her several times a week as well as being available when she needs me."

"You definitely don't need to be at her beck and call unless you want to be. I suggest that you keep your visits short and if she acts up, just leave. She will continue doing this to you unless you make the decision to set some firm boundaries for yourself. By allowing her to treat you in this way you have, in effect, given her permission to do so."

Marion stood up and held out her hand. "Good luck, Judy. If you wish to talk, come and see me again."

"Thank you," Judy tried to smile through her flowing tears.

Sitting on a bench in the hallway before she went to her mother's room, Judy made an effort to compose herself by thinking of the trip she planned to take. She knew her mother was going to blow a gasket about that too.

'In spite of all the many years of travelling she's been able to do,' Judy thought angrily, 'I know she'll begrudge me my first trip.' As anger replaced her feelings of self-pity, Judy dried the last of her tears and walked reluctantly, with feet like blocks of cement, towards her mother's room.

"Well, you finally got here. It's a long day when there's no visitors. And no one talks to me around here. They ignore me like I don't exist. You have no idea how it feels, Judy. The nurses do things for everyone else but not for me. They even took my buzzer away from me this morning. They said it was for emergencies only but their idea of an emergency and mine are two different things." Her mother greeted her with her usual long string of complaints.

"I've come every day, Mother. But I can't stay the whole day as you would like because there are so many other things I have to do too."

"Oh, I know. Everyone is always so busy. Too busy for an old woman, it seems. That has certainly been made very clear to me."

"Mother, you get a lot of visitors," Judy replied. "I'll make up a calendar so you can see how many people do come in to see you." Judy angrily ran her fingers through her untidy hair.

"Uhmff! I won't be able to read it so don't bother. It's still a long day."

"Why don't you talk to the other people in the room? Or I can bring in the newspaper for you."

"No one wants to talk to someone who is deaf," her mother complained. "And why would I want the newspaper? At my age I don't care what's in the news."

"There are a lot of interesting things in the newspaper. Or how about a book? What about getting the television?"

"I want visitors. Nothing in the newspaper has anything to do with me and I don't want to look at the television either. That's why so many old people get depression—because none of their family want to spend time with them. We get old and everyone thinks we've outlived our usefulness so we become the forgotten ones."

"Mother, you have three or four visitors almost every day. That's hardly being forgotten."

"That's duty," her mother scoffed.

"However you want to look at it, they do come," Judy said as she tried to control her growing frustration with her mother. "While we're on the subject, before you came into the hospital, I had made arrangements to go on a short vacation. I'll be leaving next week."

"While I'm sick in the hospital? I've counted on you, Judy. You're going to leave me to the abuse of these nurses? Yesterday I sat in the hall and screamed trying to get someone's attention because they don't do anything for me. No one would help me to the bathroom. They help everyone else but not me."

"But if you can get yourself out to the hall, can't you get yourself to the bathroom? Maybe they think you don't need the same help as some of the other patients require. They're understaffed and the nurses are very busy."

"Oh, I know, everyone is busy. That's all I ever hear but no one has time for an old woman anymore. There was a time when the elderly used to be respected but that time has long since passed. Now people only think about themselves."

Judy watched her mother as she ranted, a small, frail looking woman, a steel hand in a velvet glove type of person. Although in the last few years the velvet glove had become threadbare and the steel was more evident in her personality. She tried to feel some sympathy for this woman with the wrinkled flesh, the false teeth that clicked when she was angry and the veins that stood out like knotted ropes on her hands.

'I wonder how I'll feel when I get to be her age,' Judy thought. She hoped that anger wouldn't be her constant theme or that criticism and complaints her only conversation. Her mother felt that she had lived to an age where the world should revolve around her; that she was owed as much. She didn't realize, or care, that respect had to be earned. And she also failed to remember that she'd had a very good life; she was one of the fortunate ones. But she was unwilling, as long as she was alive, to allow anyone else to enjoy the same good life. She wanted everyone's world to stand still and for the family to pay homage to her because of her advanced years.

Judy sighed unhappily. 'No matter how much I do for her, it is never enough,' she thought. 'Well, no matter how guilty she tries to make me feel, I'm definitely not going to give up the opportunity of taking my first real trip.'

"I'm sorry you feel that way, Mother. Unfortunately I have to leave now. I have an appointment."

"So you spent half an hour of your precious time to visit your old mother. Is that all you can manage out of your busy schedule? And then you're going away for a week, too self-centred to care about the abuse I've been suffering. You really are an ungrateful daughter."

"I won't exactly be leaving you alone. You have three sons also, they'll be here. Now I really have to go or I'll be late. Goodbye, Mother." Judy leaned forward to kiss her mother's dry cheek but the older woman pulled away giving her daughter an angry glare instead.

Judy shrugged and walked out of the room, refusing to give in to her feelings of guilt, as she usually did. She smiled briefly as she realized that she had established her first boundary and it felt good. But the good feeling lasted only until she heard the beginnings of her mother's angry screams. Squaring her shoulders, she resolutely walked towards the elevator as the tears continued their journey down her cheeks.

# THE YOUNG GIRL
# INSIDE OF ME

I LOOK IN the mirror and see the wrinkles the years have worn in my face, the loose skin that hangs like appendages beneath my chin and the folds of flesh surrounding my eyes. Silver hair adorns my head like an unwanted old hat. The woman who stares at me from the looking glass is a stranger.

My hands, twisted with arthritis, move slowly through their tasks and my legs shuffle as I use my cane for balance. This stranger's body has betrayed me. It had once been my friend as it swung gracefully around the dance floor, ran up the stairs to a friend's house, took me canoeing and helped me win games on the tennis court. But I know, though no one else does, that a young dark-haired girl continues to reside deep within me.

That young girl can still feel the wind in her hair when she rides down Brickyard Hill on her bicycle as if it was only yesterday. Applying her brakes she comes to a screeching halt at the bottom of the hill where she quickly jumps off her bike. Although I can feel her spirit and the agility of her body as she moves, my outer shell no longer obeys my inner commands.

When I think of summers long past, I remember her excitement for the first baseball game of the season. While I sit with pain in my joints, I can still feel her sure-footed race around the bases. She stands ready on third base, her glove poised. I hear the 'whack' as the ball is hit and see it soar through the air. Her strong hands catch it and another one is out. The north island wins over the south again.

That young girl within me remembers many of the thoughts and wishes she had as she walked to school, thinking nothing of the three mile hike each way and proud of her ability to make it in under half an hour. She feels that no time has passed since she roamed the beach in search of the ornamental shells of the oyster and water-worn pieces of driftwood, leaping confidently from boulder to boulder. It seems that it was only yesterday she sat on the rocks and listened to the waves lap onto the shore while she watched seagulls swoop and squawk as they grabbed morsels of food from the orange beaks of the oyster catchers.

That girl is very much alive but she is locked within a body whose flesh is no longer firm or supple and whose movements are no longer quick. Her skin is smooth and her hair is shining while the stranger who is home to this girl lacks enthusiasm and exuberance.

When I was busier and more able-bodied and those around me valued what I had to offer, I saw only the young girl in the mirror but she no longer looks back at me; she's no longer seen by anyone, not even myself. But I know she's still there; I can feel her and hear her, and her thoughts are still mine. Late at night when the only light are the stars in the sky, we remember the friends we once knew. They are all gone, like the young girl in the mirror.

My own children are now getting their own wrinkles, thick waists and gray hair; they have aches and pains and health issues of their own. They spend their leisure time at the gym and take vitamins hoping to hold old age at bay. How did it happen that these children of mine look older than the girl within me feels? And my grandchildren, looking like my children did only yesterday, look at me like the stranger I am.

The very young look at the elderly in a different way I realized once I became aware of that stranger in the mirror. When their voices could no longer be heard by this stranger, they no longer spoke. Making an effort to be heard was like too much hard work. When stories became repeated renditions of a long life lived, they turned away in boredom. And when steps became slow and difficult, they raced ahead anxious to get where they wanted to go. The young are busy, rushing from one exciting venture to another, as the young girl within me once did. There is no time for this stranger when the world is full of places to see and explore.

The young girl within me knows when the young have no patience for the elderly. Or is it that the elderly body who has taken control only imagines what the young girl inside me can see. Perhaps it is God's little joke that the mind stays young while the body gets old. Or perhaps it is so that when the body doesn't obey, we have the young girl to remind us of what our youth had been like.

I thought about all this one spring day as I sat on a park bench watching young children play. While they tossed a ball back and forth with their companions, they laughed happily and no one noticed an old lady sitting on the bench. For them she did not appear to exist. But perhaps, I decided as I listened to their happy chatter, the old lady was only in my mind. Possibly it was only my negative feelings about ageing that had shown me the old lady in the mirror.

Ageing could be about wisdom, freedom, giving our help to others, enjoying life, doing what we've always wanted to do, volunteering for a worthy cause or, working towards a long forgotten dream. Ageing didn't have to be empty days filled with nothing. My mind, the young girl within me decided, wasn't going to stagnate. My days were going to be full again.

I suddenly remembered my long ago dream. It wasn't too late I decided as I got up from the bench. I hardly felt my arthritis I realized as I smiled at the children. They responded with smiles of their own. I swung my cane as I walked along the winding paths where flowers grew in a variety of brilliant abundance. Cocky little finches fluttered from branch to branch singing cheerful tunes grateful that the last of winter was in full retreat.

The young girl inside me laughed, as I was doing. I no longer felt old. I had a purpose and a plan. "Hello Henry," I called to the green grocer. "Do you have any brussel sprouts today?"

"Hello, Mrs. Miller. I haven't seen you looking so well for a long time. Did you discover the fountain of youth?"

"I haven't felt so well for some time. Isn't it funny how the mind can play tricks on us? If we think we're old, we'll feel old."

"I guess so. I haven't much thought about it. But I do have brussels sprouts. Are you entertaining this evening?"

"That's a wonderful idea. I think it's exactly what I'll do. I used to have dinner parties almost every week but haven't for a long time. I'll have to get more things now. Can you deliver them, Henry?"

"It would be my pleasure. Would you like a ride home also? You've got yourself quite a long way to go."

"Thank you, Henry but I think I'll walk. I haven't seen such a beautiful day in a long, long time. It would be a shame to waste it, don't you agree?"

"That I do, that I do, Mrs. Miller."

"And Henry, if you ever see an old man in the mirror, he only exists in your mind. Stay in close contact with the young person inside of you."

"Ah yes, Mrs. Miller. I will certainly do that."

As we walked home on that beautiful spring day, the young girl inside of me said, "Good for you. You were ready to give up on living instead of enjoying life; you were bowing out too early. I'm glad you realized that you are only as old as you think you are. You didn't remember that I used to say that everything is a state of mind."

I had to agree with her. She's one smart young lady.

# BIRTH OF A WOMAN

ELIZA, AT NINETEEN years of age, had not as yet been born. Shyly looking around at others her own age, she knew she did not exist. Not as they existed. No one ever really saw her. She knew because their eyes slid quickly over her. Nor did they hear her when she occasionally made an effort to speak. And on most days she could feel the vacuum that surrounded her as it pulled her into its vortex and, screaming to be released, she was heard by no one.

When rarely she was spoken to and asked a question, she had no answer because she seldom had an opinion. Words managed to escape her tongue as she searched frantically through the partial phrases and incomplete thoughts that tumbled around inside her head, looking for the correct thing to say. By the time she discovered something that she deemed intelligent from the various thoughts that cluttered her head, the need to say it had long since past and she was quickly forgotten when a more interesting person approached, someone who had an opinion, who looked them in the face, who knew they were as good as anyone else. Eliza knew she fit into neither of these categories. She was a nonentity in the eyes of herself as well as to others.

Other young women had self-esteem and self-confidence. They walked with their heads held high, laughter on their faces and happiness in their eyes. She, however, saw only her feet as she scurried to wherever she had to go. Hoping to remain unnoticed, she was seen by few.

Eliza's smile was gentle when rarely it showed, her posture submissive. Her body language screamed her beliefs about herself to the world. No "I want" or "I think" would ever have escaped her lips even had there been a stick of dynamite in her mouth to force the words out.

But during her young adult years there began to be a gradual change. She wasn't exactly sure when the change had come about or why? But one day the cloud that had surrounded her most of her life lifted and the world looked slightly brighter.

Taking a good look at herself in the mirror one day, she realized that her appearance had altered somewhat since she'd last really taken the time to observe how she looked. She hadn't noticed that some time in the last little while her hair had developed nice waves and the color was much nicer than she had previously thought. She had thought it to be mousy brown but she now noticed that it had strands of gold in it where it caught the sunlight.

'My eyes aren't bad either,' she decided with a small smile. She had thought they were an indefinite color but as she continued to stare into the mirror, she saw shades of green and yes, there was a sparkle to them that had never been there before. And her mouth when she smiled was really quite pleasing. Her lower lip was full but not too much so. She had previously thought her lips were nothing more than a straight line separating the top portion of her face from the lower section. She noticed too that her cheekbones, ones she had often thought were too prominent, now seemed to fit the contours of her face. She began to practice smiling in the mirror so that now she saw an entirely different person than the one that had previously looked back at her.

While her confidence improved, based on her mirror's reflection, Eliza now looked very carefully at the people she passed everyday on her way to work. Smiling tentatively at a stranger, she was surprised when she was rewarded with a smile. 'She saw me,' Eliza thought happily to herself.

Saying "hello" to a passerby, she was greeted by a friendly face. "Hi", she said to a young girl walking by her side, "how are you today?"

"I'm fine. How are you? Are you going to work?"

"Yes. Are you on your way to school?" She smiled at the young girl with a mouth that she now knew was not an ugly slash across her face.

Hurrying home that evening she realized that she could be like the other young women she saw each day. She could be born a woman of worth in her own eyes and perhaps in the eyes of others as well. Up until then she had not valued the person she was. She had been too critical of who she had thought she was, and she was beginning to suspect, more so than anyone else may possibly have been.

During Eliza's whole life she had always emphasized her own weaknesses rather than appreciating her strengths. She hadn't realized that in every human being there are strong and weak points and that the weaknesses could be made into strengths. She reluctantly realized also that she wouldn't have been human had she had no weak points since not one of us is perfect. She had expected perfection in herself but had overlooked the imperfections of others, seeing none when many existed.

As she gradually realized that she had an opportunity to be more than she had thought herself to be, her inner tears turned to laughter on the outside and with each small step towards self-confidence, her perception of herself changed. As her perception of herself changed, so then did others' perception of her change also. Each time she smiled at a stranger, and received a friendly smile in return, she felt an inner glow and a further strengthening of her confidence. She was slowly beginning to realize that she was just as deserving of love and respect as anyone else.

She began to notice that others were not the perfections of humanity she had always assumed them to be. She began to see the frailties of human nature. She saw those who were dishonest, who lied, who did not treat others well and still others who because they thought so well of themselves, others did too. These were often the people she had looked up to in the past. In many cases they were the ones who had made her feel less than she was. With a rueful shake of her head, she thought, 'I was the only one who could do that. I can't blame anyone else.'

As she became positive, optimistic, cheerful and exuded a growing assertiveness, Eliza was allowing herself to be the person she was born to be. As she began to walk with a smile on her lips and with her head held high, her hair bouncing freely on her shoulders as she walked, she became approachable. People began to ask her opinion. She was surprised to find that she now had worthwhile opinions that she could share with others. She could now make choices without the agony of indecision. People began to notice her. No longer did their eyes slide over her as if she was of no consequence. Self-esteem began to have new meaning as it related to herself. She realized she was being born as a new woman. It was a rebirth, an opportunity to begin anew.

Eliza contemplated her attributes, never before considering that there had been any to contemplate. How could she not have seen the possibilities and her potential before this?

During her rebirth, Eliza thought often about the new woman she was becoming. The birth had been a long and painful process, as most births are. But she was now a woman who knew she deserved more than what she had previously allowed herself to believe she should have.

She knew she had potential but the question was, where could she go from here? She knew she could do and be anything she wanted to be but what? What had she learned from her whole experience? The only limitations would be those she imposed upon herself.

'That is a rather daunting thought,' she mused as she smiled to herself. 'But I can be whoever I want to be.' The thought gave her a satisfactory feeling, a completely alien feeling to what she had been familiar with before her rebirth.

She considered the idea and wondered why anyone would impose limitations on themselves? 'But haven't I been doing that my whole life before I was born again?" she asked herself? Closing her eyes she saw the woman that had existed before her rebirth.

The old Eliza had walked with her head held down, never looking anyone directly in the face. She spoke rarely and when occasionally words were spoken, they were indistinct. She never participated in anything involving a group and had only one friend who she allowed to do most of the talking. Eliza had thought she didn't mind. 'After all,' she reminded herself, 'I don't like to be the center of attention.' She realized now that it was because she thought she had nothing to offer. She hadn't respected herself. She was coming to realize that there were probably many like her who felt the same way.

The difference, she realized now was that the new Eliza didn't concern herself so much with what other people thought about her because it was more important what she thought about herself. She liked herself. She respected herself. As her new self grew, she realized that now she really listened to what people said instead of worrying about what she would say if someone happened to ask her. She had become more outward looking rather than inward looking. She became more interested in what was happening around her rather than what was happening within herself. She asked others questions and became interested in their answers and in their lives. She became more 'other' oriented rather than 'me' oriented.

The more 'other' oriented Eliza became, the happier she was. She discovered that some of the young women who had seemed to be so self-confident actually had insecurities of their own, as all people do. They just hadn't let it dominate their lives as she had done.

Eliza realized in her rebirth experience that every person can become the person they want to become if they are determined enough to do it. She now understood that she could be happy if she wanted to be, or she could choose to be sad. She could be friendly and outgoing or she could be shy and withdrawn. She could have as many friends as she wanted, if she wanted to be a friend. She could have good relationships if she wanted to make an effort in her relationships.

Everyone, she realized, also has within them the potential to become what they want to be. We can be lawyers, doctors, nurses or teachers. Or we can be writers, artists or gardeners. Eliza realized that there was nothing to stop her from accomplishing all of her dreams, if she really wanted them. Anything she wanted to do was up to her to achieve. The sky was the limit.

'The question remains,' she reminded herself one early Spring morning, 'what do I want to achieve? Or what do I want to become based on what I have learned?' She glanced around at the trees forming new bright green buds on their branches and the season's early flowers poking their fragile heads through the protective earth. Eliza's eyes, as they looked at the wonders of Spring's surrounding beauty, rested on a young girl of about twelve years old sitting shyly on the bus bench. Her body language screamed to all who could see her, 'I am worthless, I am nothing.'

Eliza approached the girl with a smile on her face. "Hello, my name is Eliza." The girl offered a fleeting smile and looked at the ground, her face a crimson mask.

"What is your name?" Eliza asked. The girl's mumbled words were unintelligible and Eliza knew in that instant how other people had felt when confronted with herself a short time ago. But they hadn't been reborn.

"There was a time when I felt just as you do," Eliza smiled at the girl. "I found it difficult to talk to others. My shyness was a shield surrounding me, I used it as my excuse not to talk to others and then, a strange thing happened."

The girl slowly looked up. "What happened?"

"I was born again. I finally realized that I was as good as anyone else."

A puzzled expression crossed the girl's young face. "How?"

"I look at you and see a very pretty girl. Has anyone ever told you how pretty you are?"

The girl shook her head and Eliza saw tears begin to form in the shallow pools of her eyes.

"Well, you are. You have lovely hair, like corn silk. And your eyes are a beautiful shade of blue like the water in the Sea of Cortez. When you go home today, look in your mirror and I'll bet you'll see those things for yourself. Then try smiling at your reflection and it'll smile back at you, just as anyone else you smile at will do. And I'll bet my bottom dollar that you're smart too," Eliza said.

"That's the problem," the young girl muttered. "The kids say I'm a nerd."

"I have a feeling if you smile at the other children, and join in their games and laughter, they won't think you're a nerd."

"There's my bus," the girl said with a fleeting smile and, with a slight wave of her hand, she was gone.

Eliza sat watching the bus as it rolled down the street when an idea came to her. 'I can help young children become more confident, have self-esteem and, to feel good about themselves,' she thought excitedly. 'That will be my mission.'

As she boarded her own bus, she considered what she'd have to do to put herself into the position of being able to help children who were shy in a way that destroyed their lives and limited who they could be.

Watching birds fly from one blossom-covered tree to another, their cheerful chirping filling the warm morning air, Eliza knew exactly what she had to do. 'I'll do it,' she told herself determinedly. 'I don't want other children growing up to be adults with a feeling of worthlessness.' She sighed and smiled at the elderly lady walking down the aisle of the bus. It felt good to have a purpose.

# FREE COMPOST

---

WAKING LATE AND feeling guilty about a wasted day, Heidi decided to borrow her son's truck to take advantage of the free compost she had recently seen advertised at a local nursery.

Holding her pounding head, the results of a hangover, she stared at the large mound of compost. "How much would you like, Ma'am?" The man looked down on her from his perch on the backhoe, a quizzical look on his sunburned face.

"Oh, fill it up," she replied with a feeble attempt at a smile. "I have quite a large garden area to do."

Eyebrows raised he asked, "Are you sure?"

With an attempt at a nod, she winced and watched while the backhoe filled her truck with all the wonderful compost she was sure would give her a bumper crop of vegetables and beautiful flowers. She could hardly wait to get home with it. Then she'd crawl back into bed, she silently decided.

"There you go," he said, continuing to shake his head as he finished putting the last shovel full of compost into the truck.

Approaching the pick-up, her eyes started to water. "What is that awful smell?" she gasped.

"Pig manure, Ma'am."

"Pig manure? I thought it was compost."

"It is compost, Ma'am like I told you; pig manure."

"I can't take that home. My neighbors will kill me, not to mention my son."

"Well, I can't take it out of your truck with this," he said indicating the huge backhoe.

"What am I going to do?" she wailed as nausea began to creep towards her throat.

Shrugging he moved off to help another excited customer. She wondered briefly whether she should warn the poor unsuspecting man but didn't have the energy to do so. It was slowly beginning to dawn on her that the smell permeating the air, and which she had earlier

---

discounted as coming from a nearby farm, was in fact emanating from that pile of compost.

After considering her dilemma, she unhappily backed up to the huge pile and began shovelling the now 'not so wonderful compost' back onto the mound of still unclaimed treasure. Grumbling to herself as she shovelled, she knew she was only doing this because she had never been one to give up on a project and besides she reluctantly had to admit, she really had very few other options available to her. In a nauseous, angry way she was proud of her strong-minded principles.

But the more she shovelled the compost, the more it appeared to multiply right there on the back of her truck and the weaker her principles became. She tried calling her sons, she tried phoning her daughter, she even tried phoning her mother, for heaven sakes all to no avail. It was as if they all knew she was out there shovelling pig manure.

Finally completely overcome with nausea as a result of the 'free compost', she realized she was probably not the nurseries' best advertisement as she gagged into the surrounding shrubbery. But not letting it stop her, she continued to stand on top of that damned pile of manure shovelling it back onto the pile from whence it came.

Eventually another pick-up pulled in beside her. Putting on her best smiling face she greeted the newcomers and extolled the virtues of free compost. By now though her face was a pale shade of what it had once been and her freckles stood out like boulders on a white sandy beach. After explaining her dilemma, and with difficulty holding back her threatening tears while also managing to control her gag reflexes, she convinced them to take some off her truck. She smiled happily for a brief moment.

"Well, I can take a little but I don't need that much," the fellow said. However, his 'little' didn't amount to much of a dent.

After what seemed like hours of, 'I wish I was in bed wasting my day' shovelling and a few more bouts of nausea, a kindly gentleman pulled in beside her. Again she patiently explained her dilemma, and he, kind soul that he was, suggested he could unload the rest of her truck at his place if she followed him there. With three-quarters of the compost still in the back of the truck she would have been prepared to follow him to Australia if she had to. As she followed his pick-up, eager to leave the nauseous fumes behind, she had completely lost any interest in a garden of any kind, let alone a large one. Perhaps grassing the area, she thought as she drove, would be an excellent alternative.

On arrival at their destination, it took her only a matter of minutes to realize that his wife was not pleased to see her, or the truckload of manure. "Well," Heidi confided to her in an effort at friendship, "I'm not very pleased with the manure myself but it's amazing what men get excited about, isn't it." She managed to smile into the glowering face in spite of the threatening nausea. The woman barely responded, unable to remove her eyes from the boulders on Heidi's face.

As Heidi pulled out of the driveway, she heaved a sigh of relief while she forced the bile back down her throat. The truck was finally empty and only the smell of the wonders of nature remained of her week-end adventure and her effort not to waste a day.

But with one look at her son's face, she realized the day was not yet over. With one very small sniff, he glared at her and declared his truck would be off-limits to her in the future. With tears spilling down her face, she was a little hurt that he hadn't appreciated her well-intended efforts.

The moral of the story is: Don't worry about a wasted day in bed. We all deserve one.

# A CHILD'S CHRISTMAS WISH

H IS EYES LARGE, his blonde hair shimmering under the photographer's bright lamp, he smiled shyly at Santa. At two and a half years old, he looked tiny on the white-bearded man's lap.

"What would you like Santa to bring you for Christmas?" the large man asked.

"A choo-choo train and rocks and sticks," he whispered.

"Uh, yes, a choo-choo train." Santa rubbed his gloved hand thoughtfully over his cheek. "Rocks and sticks too?" Santa's face wore a puzzled expression.

The small child nodded his head emphatically, "Yes, rocks and sticks."

"Well, I'm sure that can be arranged," Santa smiled as he handed him a candy cane and coloring book and lifted him down from his lap.

For the next few weeks the child talked of little else except the rocks and sticks he was going to get from Santa for Christmas. His excitement seemed to know no bounds. But did he really want rocks and sticks or was it only a momentary passing fancy?

Right up until Christmas Eve, his parents weren't sure how to handle this delicate situation. Finally by late that evening they had made their decision.

Early Christmas morning, they gave him the brightly wrapped box of rocks and sticks. As he tore off the colorful paper and opened the box, he beamed. "Rocks and sticks!"

As he inspected each specimen carefully, his parents encouraged him to open his other gifts. Reluctantly, he finally put his precious gift aside and opened the box holding his 'choo-choo' train.

For the rest of Christmas Day he interspersed his playtime between the train and the rocks and sticks. "Why don't you open your other gifts?" his parents asked throughout the day.

"No," he announced as he happily continued to play with these two precious gifts; the gifts Santa had said he would bring.

This story is true; the little boy is my grandson. As I think about his joy at receiving rocks and sticks, I realize that as adults we place too much importance on the dollar value of gifts. We do not need to buy a child expensive toys. Many of these toys have been hyped by television but in fact have very little play value once the novelty has worn off. The rocks and sticks were played with in more imaginary ways than many toys off a department store shelf could be. This was also an example to all of us that children don't need to have a lot of gifts under the tree either in order to be happy.

When I thought further about his boundless happiness with his box of rocks and sticks, I realized that children have a far better understanding of the meaning of Christmas than we do as adults. As we grow older, many people estimate the value of a gift based on its cost.

This year as a family we decided to cut back on our Christmas spending. We didn't cut back on our gift-giving but did make the decision to give smaller gifts because the thought itself is the most important.

It took a two and a half year old child to remind us that happiness comes from within; it is being pleased with the simple things in life. Many of us forget the importance of this.

# A VACATION WITH
# GRANDPA

---

T HEIR FAMILY VACATION was going to start out like any other normal vacation with two grandparents and three grandchildren about to embark on a three week trip. Except that their friends didn't think it was normal at all. "Three grandchildren?" they asked as their eyes did acrobatics inside their sockets. "Are you crazy?" Isabella wasn't sure herself but suspected that by the end of three weeks, there would be a story to tell.

They drove four long, hot days with no air conditioning in the hottest weather any of them could imagine. The children, unbelievably complained not at all but the lone adult male who had insisted that the malfunctioning air conditioner would not be a problem, and therefore refused to spend the money to have it fixed, whined the entire four days. Taking a day each to drive through Washington and Oregon and two days through California, it was not until they had almost reached their destination before a little voice finally asked, "Are we almost there yet, Nana?" 'Three grandchildren,' Isabella thought, 'all better behaved than their grandfather.'

As the family pulled in front of Isabella's brother's home in Arizona where they were going to spend a week, Grandpa misjudged the outside overhang of the motorhome and knocked the mailbox onto the sidewalk. The cement base lay in crumbled little pieces on the ground while the three uncomplaining children and Isabella carefully stepped over it leaving Grandpa muttering angrily beside the motorhome, blaming the tin box for the mess on the ground.

Isabella thought often about her friends' references to being crazy for taking three grandchildren while she and the children frolicked in the swimming pool and her husband cursed for the two days it took him to rebuild the cement base to its 'almost' original state. She wondered if it had been crazy to bring the husband when he stubbornly refused to enjoy the pool or sit on the patio when the evening had cooled preferring to sulk inside instead guzzling the beer he seemed to prefer to the company of his wife and well-behaved grandchildren.

At the end of the week they drove to Anaheim for four lovely, hot, fun-filled days of walking around Disneyland waiting their chance to go on Thunder Mountain, Space Mountain and the Hollywood Tower of Terror. But at the last minute Grandpa decided that wasn't his thing and he'd rather sit around inside the motorhome, in a hot parking lot, with no air conditioning. So Isabella set off with the three children in tow. At this point she wasn't sure who was the crazy one, she or Grandpa.

After four enjoyable days in Disneyland, the family set off for Arizona in 48 degree weather with no air conditioner, their faces turning bright red from the heat. Isabella grumbled that he could have had it fixed as he had languished in the overheated motorhome while they were Soaring Over California or exploring Adventure Land. But Grandpa had decided that after this trip, they may not need it again. So like troopers they persevered in the heat as they made their way to the Grand Canyon, the children complaining not at all. Through deserts and over mountains they travelled until finally they stopped near a small town, hoping to find a campsite. But once stopped, the motorhome wouldn't start again. Isabella laughed and her husband glowered.

"What's so funny?" he asked with a tad touch of testiness to his voice.

"It's our lucky day," she declared.

"How so?" he asked grumpily.

"Well, we could have broken down in the middle of nowhere."

"We are in the middle of nowhere, Nana," one grandson pointed out in a quiet voice.

"But it's not as 'nowhere' as it could have been," she told him with a smile. "We're very, very close to a campsite, almost walking distance really. But just give it time, it'll start again."

"What makes you think so?" Grandpa asked. "I'd hardly call you a mechanic."

"Since we don't have another option other than waiting, we'll soon find out, won't we."

And still the grandchildren didn't complain as they waited beside the roadway and eventually it did start again. When they arrived at the

Grand Canyon, the children were awe-struck at the sight. "There is nothing to compare to it," Isabella enthused. The children agreed that it was well worth the trip in 48 degree weather, more when you consider the additional heat when travelling in a tin can. Grandpa wasn't quite as enthusiastic about the gorgeous view preferring to hang tight to his grumpy persona.

'They were definitely not crazy to be bringing those charming little people,' Isabella thought to herself. But Grandpa was still on a roll with his misjudges. While they were leaving their campsite the following morning, Isabella's husband failed to notice a tree stump and tore the corner out of their motorhome. It was the corner that housed the secondary battery that the fridge ran on while they were driving. Well what the heck—warm drinks, melted freezies and canned meals are better than nothing. One mustn't quibble about the little things. And once again the children adjusted well to drinking warm drinks, far better than Grandpa did to drinking his warm beer.

After a stop at Bryce Canyon in Utah, another unbelievable sight, they arrived at their campsite. When they tried to hook up their water supply, they ended up with water all over the bathroom floor. It was a loose connection without the appropriate tools to fix it. And because Grandpa didn't want to have it fixed in American funds, Isabella, with the help of those wonderful grandchildren, used pots and kettles to bring water into the motorhome. It was just like camping in the 'good old days' only better, Isabella decided, because at least they didn't have to sleep on the ground. Not yet, at least. Grandpa was still on a roll.

From there they travelled to Nevada where they stopped at Virginia City. Another great place to visit and one that Isabella and the children decided they'd like to go back to again when the motorhome was in a little better shape. And perhaps without Grandpa, Isabella thought as she looked at her husband's grumpy visage and thought about his latest escapade that happened when they had pulled into their campsite in Virginia City.

Isabella had asked her husband if he would like her to direct him while he backed up. "No," he replied tersely, "it'll be fine. I can do it."

Following the sudden stop and the sound of grinding metal, she realized that she shouldn't have listened to this man who didn't have a great track record so far. She should have risked life and limb and jumped out of their moving RV because within minutes he had 'somehow' attached himself to a metal fence post. That wasn't too bad though. The problem was when he tried to pull away and the bumper and part of the back wall of the motorhome came away also. But a few well-placed nails and colorful words fixed that.

The children were looking better all the time, they were fabulous, not an ounce of trouble. But grandpa on the other hand . . . Well from hereon out it will be Grandma and the grandchildren. Travelling with Grandpa was just too darn hard.

# A NEW HOME FOR GRANDMA

JEFFERSON AND KIMBERLEY had been worried about Grandma's well-being since her stay in the hospital last June. Living in the suite below them, they knew she'd never fully regained her health and, in fact since Christmas, had seemed to be steadily deteriorating. It was becoming a concern, not only for them but also for the whole family. As she required more and more help, the whole family realized that it was quickly becoming necessary to make the decision to put her on an assisted living list.

After talking to her son, and knowing also the degree of care her mother needed because she was doing much of it, Cheryl contacted the Seniors' Health Department to get her mother assessed.

Grandma, when it was explained to her, was not happy about the necessity for such a move even though she had begun to realize the necessity for it also. But in spite of her continuing difficulties, Grandma hoped that a call would not come for a couple of years even though both Jefferson and Kimberley, and Cheryl knew she would require more care long before that.

In the previous months, Grandma had spent about six weeks over a period of time with Cheryl because of her arthritis flare-ups and other health-related problems. "I really can't do this," Cheryl confided to her son. "It is so hard to get her up the stairs to the bedroom and once she's up there, it's too difficult for her to go up and down again, even with my help so it means she's stuck up there. And then she calls me constantly to do something for her so I'm up and down all day long."

"You can't look after her, Mom. That's not good for her or for you," Jefferson said.

"She can be very difficult and bad tempered. At one point when she was with me, I threatened that I was going to take her back to the hospital."

"I've seen her be difficult when she doesn't get her own way. Now that we've got the new baby, we can't be running up and down the stairs all the time either. She has even called us at two a.m. because she wanted me to do something for her. And it wasn't anything that couldn't have waited until morning. She just happened to be awake and didn't consider that we wouldn't be also."

"I've been phoning to remind her about taking her medication but I can't be sure that she is taking it. And I can't be running over twice a day—that's forty minutes each way. My place isn't set up for her with the problems she has and nor is there room for all the stuff she feels is a necessity to bring with her. I know she wants to live with me."

"That isn't feasible, Mom. And you don't have to feel guilty, she needs to be some place where they can give her some of the extra help she needs. As far as I can see, the assisted living accommodation is the only possible alternative."

"I'll take her out looking at places. I know there is a waiting list for most of them."

The call came three months after Grandma went on the list. Cheryl started to help her downsize but it was not an easy task. Grandma had kept things from the 1920's and 1930's and her 1400 square foot basement suite was stuffed almost to the rafters.

"She wants to take everything. I keep reminding her that she's going from a two bedroom place to a bachelor apartment. But she's finding things she forgot she had and now thinks she can't live without them," Cheryl told her son.

"The best thing is probably to take over what she actually needs and what doesn't fit, we'll find homes for. I know she won't like that."

"Not at all. I was going through her closets with her yesterday. She's a size 8 now since she lost all that weight. She has clothes that are size 16 and 18 that no longer fit her. You can tell by just looking at them even if you didn't look at the label to see what size they were but she insisted on trying on everything in that closet. Some of the outfits she insisted she wanted to keep regardless of the size made her look like the neighborhood bag lady."

"I've seen her closets. She's got three of them full and many of the clothes still have the price tags on them, I've noticed."

"I know and if I said something was much too large, or I haven't seen her wear that for years, her reply was that it was her favorite or she wanted to keep it for sentimental reasons. I finally told her she didn't have room for so many sentimental reasons.

"Yes, she told Kimberley that you were making her get rid of all of her favorite things. I thought I would try to help too last evening. In her cedar chest she had two fur coats that she insisted she wanted to keep. I have never seen her wear either one of them. When I mentioned it, she said that doesn't mean she wants to get rid of them. When she was in the bathroom, I took them upstairs. I hate doing it but you have to admit, Mom, she is a hoarder."

"She always has been but as she's gotten older, she's gotten worse. She found a fur wrap with a matching pill box hat stuffed into a plastic bag in the corner of her closet and was thrilled. She said I think I'll wear this fur wrap down to dinner. I told her that it wasn't exactly a country club. And to further back up my argument, I told her that people hate people who wear fur coats. She reluctantly agreed to give it up but she insisted that she was still going to keep her mink jacket."

"Oh, I didn't know about that one. I've never seen her wear any of them. Why have them if they're just going to be stuffed into the closet?"

"And that's just her clothes. Then there are her collections of dog ornaments, postcards, stamps, spoons, dog calendars going back many, many years, albums of pictures of stranger's dogs, records, albums of pictures of castles she's cut out of magazines, a roomful of geneology binders, all filled with ancestors, shelves and shelves of books, an abundance of vases (not really a collection, just a bunch), and tons and tons of 'just stuff'. And when I pulled out what was under her bed, there was a whole collection of musical instruments, none of which she plays."

"Really? What kind?"

"There was the violin and the mandolin which belonged to my father. The harpsichord and the zither were instruments she wanted to learn years ago but never got around to and there's the guitar which she wanted to learn also and a keyboard. But the piano that she does know how to play, she never does."

"If she didn't mind I'd like to look at some of them," Jefferson smiled sheepishly at his mother.

"I'll mention that to her. She doesn't have room for them though so they can't go with her. There was also some silverware, still in their plastic wraps, mostly tarnished. It had probably been there for years. She didn't remember having it but was excited when she saw it. She said it would be good for all the company she was going to have. She's made no effort to have company in all the years she's been here."

"Poor you Mom. We know how difficult she can be on a regular day. I couldn't imagine trying to help her eliminate and sort.

"It's been a painful process, I'm sure as much for her as for me. In spite of the fact that she is coming to realize that everything is just not going to fit into a studio apartment, she still snaps, yells and demands and in general is not very pleasant if I suggest she part with something. To say she is not a happy person is an understatement. I told her that I can understand her feelings of loss. 'But what are your options?' I asked her. I couldn't think of any and nor could she."

"The actual move day is going to be very difficult for her," Jefferson said with a shake of his head.

"If we, and some of the others in the family do the moving and get things as set up as possible, and if perhaps Kimberley and a couple of the other girls take her for lunch so we can get her things moved in without her making things more difficult for us, it might not be too bad."

"Good idea. It definitely would make the move easier if she wasn't here."

"After things are in, I'll make her bed, get the things set up in her kitchen, the fridge and the bathroom and get as much unpacked as I can while you all move the big things. Then later maybe we can all go out for dinner. I'll go back the next day and finish unpacking and putting away the rest of her things."

"How long do you think it'll take?" Jefferson asked as he looked around at the piles of boxes.

"I don't know. That will be the least of it. Look at the rest of this stuff. She has been hoarding this stuff for years. What are we going to do with it all? She's been stockpiling things she has absolutely no use for. What a waste of money. She keeps saying it's because she lived through the Depression but to my knowledge, they didn't have money to waste then. You'd think the experience of the Depression would translate into her saving money."

"How does Grandma like her new place?" Jefferson asked his mother.

"I asked her that when I took her for lunch yesterday. She said her new place is very cozy. She likes it and she feels relieved that she no longer has to cook her meals, do any housework or even make her own bed. She has commented several times on how well they look after the residents. She enjoys the company of women her own age and will be able to take advantage of all of the recreation that is offered, once she gets settled in. She has decided this was probably a good move and seems to have come to terms with the loss of her stuff. She said to me, "I don't know why I thought I needed it all.""

# HER WAY OR THE HIGHWAY

FREDERICK WALKED SLOWLY through the cemetery. His father's grave site was along the back row near the tall cedar hedge that separated the cemetery from the busy street. It was a quiet area and he always felt a sense of tranquillity as he walked through the headstones in spite of the sadness cemeteries evoked. He looked at the new graves with their abundance of fresh flowers and wondered how long it would be before they began to look like most of the other plots, barren of anything that signified a once cared for and loved family member.

He thought of his mother and father's headstones placed companionably side by side in a way they had never been in life. Frederick visited his father's grave at least once a month bringing flowers to lay on the mound during the winter months and planting colourful reminders of life during the summer months. As he approached the spot where his father lay, he was glad he remembered to bring scissors to trim the grass that was encroaching into the area of brightly colored flowers. He felt a slight twinge of guilt when he looked over to his mother's grass-covered and unadorned resting place. He, like everyone, knew there was a reason for it. One only had to look at the inscription, 'Margaret Frances Robertson, Her Way or the Highway' on her headstone, to know the answer. The headstone, he noticed, was beginning to become slightly green with the passing of the winters that she had lain there.

Those looking at it, who did not know their mother, might wonder at a family that would allow their mother's last resting place to forever bear those words but her daily words to her husband had always been, "Jonathan, don't you know by now that it's my way or the highway so get with the program."

'We all knew,' Frederick thought, 'we didn't need the constant reminder.' They also knew that their father said little, not wishing to provoke his wife and create chaos within the family.

Frederick carefully clipped the grass and dead headed the flowers and left a note as he often did in the buried container near the headstone. It was his way of feeling connected to his father—a man who had deserved to be treated better by his wife than he was. A man who had suffered without complaint and who treated all who he came in contact with with consideration and respect. He was a man who gave his time and while he lived, showed a vast ability for unconditional love for his whole family.

As a father, his patience had no boundaries, his wisdom no limits and his smiles were constant. When there was a problem, he was there, when there were tears, he knew exactly what to say, and when anyone screwed up, he knew how to make it right. His family came first and they all knew it. When he died, there was standing room only in the chapel and many of his friends got up to say how they felt about him. When he died, the world lost a very special person and the family was never the same. His grandchildren mourned him as much as his children did. He had been such a big part of everyone's life.

Frederick gazed at his father's headstone and smiled at the inscription as he ran his fingers lovingly over the rough surface. 'There Was None Better, Jonathon Frederick Robertson, Forever Loved and Missed By All'.

Reaching into the container with the messages he pulled them out and slowly began to read them. The first one dated November 17th had been written less than a month after his father's untimely death. Frederick's eyes clouded with memories as he read it. 'Dad, You have left an emptiness in all our lives. I know that in time this void will fill with memories and we'll once again be able to laugh as we did when you sat in our midst. I think often of your sparkling eyes and smile that welcomed others. You are with us always. Love from your son, Frederick.'

Opening another one dated almost a year later, he read, 'Dad, you came to me in a dream last night. You came out of the mists at the end of a pier and walking towards me, you had a smile on your face and your arms reached towards me. I started to run towards the pier and when I had almost reached your side, you disappeared, back into the mists, from where you came. I woke up and was not able to go back to sleep again. Your loss is still felt deeply but we know that you are now without pain and for that we are happy. We love you, Your son, Frederick.'

Frederick glanced across at his mother's tombstone and saw the blurred image of her face, the deep furrows of discontent pulling her mouth down and the grooves creating ridges between her eyebrows. Her eyes did not sparkle and her mouth wore an habitual grimace instead of a smile. She wore negativity like a halo and rainclouds loomed daily. Her voice was not the sound of sweet angels but of rusted hinges like those on an old barn door. He wracked his thoughts to think of what kind of note he could leave his mother. It would have to be something that told her that all the bad she foretold for the future had not come to fruition. He had done very well in life, as they all had. She would be surprised; she had expected nothing of any of them. He would have liked her to know of their successes in spite of her lack of encouragement. And it had all been due to their father.

Looking down at the notes in his hand, he opened another one dated the previous summer. 'Dad, So many years have passed since you left us in body but you are with us always in our thoughts. We have so many wonderful memories of your kindness, thoughtfulness, laughter and love. Even those of your grandchildren who did not know you when you were alive feel your presence with us. They all know what a great husband, father and grandfather you were. You have been a role model to all of us. I am proud of our whole family but you lay the groundwork, you paved the way for all of us to become who we are. We have much to thank you for. I am sure that even as your grandchildren become parents, they will tell the story to their children about the wonderful man you were. With lots of love from your son, Frederick.'

Putting the note back into the container with the rest of them, Frederick took a piece of paper and pen from the inside pocket of his jacket. Smoothing the paper onto his knee, he wrote, 'Mother, I have not left you a note before this because it has been difficult to know what to write. It is as difficult in death as it was when you were alive. I feel sad that you were unable to appreciate the joys of motherhood as much as I enjoy being a parent. We, your children lost out on having a loving mother, but you probably lost more than we did. For so many years I wondered why? I think I now know the answer. I believe it was because you were unable to love yourself, you were unable to love others. I think there must have been many times when you were very lonely and for that I wish I knew then what I now suspect. Mother, I hope you are happier now, wherever you are, than you ever were in life.'

Re-reading the note, he slowly added, 'Your son, Frederick.' Finding a stick, he began to dig in the soft earth on his mother's grave site. Drying out the inside of the jar that he had used to carry water in for the flowers, with a tissue, he placed the note inside and put the jar into the hole. Sitting back, he looked into the distance and thought of the sadness that was probably his mother's life.

'Things change and holding grudges benefits no one. Maybe,' he thought as he looked at the tombstone, 'we could get a new one with a different inscription. She was who she was because of her background.' Frederick thought about his grandparents on his mother's side and realized he probably didn't have to look any further than that. Perhaps the inscription instead could read: 'I knew no other way, I tried the best I could.' Maybe after all these years, it was time to cut his mother some slack.

# THE ENGAGEMENTS

"W HY ARE YOU doing this?" Michelle asked her mother, fury contorting her face.

"And why not, Michelle?" Nancy stared into her daughter's angry blue eyes. She really didn't quite understand her daughter's angry outburst. She could understand maybe a slight annoyance and perhaps even some confusion. She felt somewhat confused herself at the change in the road her life had taken but she didn't feel that it should have resulted in this much anger from her only daughter.

"Why? Mother, how could you even ask? It's not right. Don't you realize what this will mean?"

"Of course I realize what it means, dear. But there is nothing illegal or immoral about it. Unorthodox, possibly. But no one can hang me for being unorthodox."

"Don't dear me. Don't you realize that if you go ahead with this foolishness, we will be sister-in-laws. That is absolutely ludicrous."

"Dear, it is unusual but it is not ludicrous. Nancy was beginning to feel the first bit of irritation but she was not going to give her daughter the satisfaction of knowing she was upset. She didn't feel that it was the horrific situation her daughter seemed to think it was.

"What would I call you? And even worse, what would my children call you? Aunt Nancy? We'll be laughing stocks. Actually, I do think probably you would be more than me but you are less concerned than I am. What is the matter with you?"

"There is nothing the matter with me, dear. I don't think it's such a huge problem. I really think you're exaggerating the whole issue, Michelle."

"I . . . don't . . . think . . . so," Michelle spat out.

"I have an idea," Nancy said with a try at logic. "Why don't we get the opinion of both Craig and Connor?"

"Why bring them into it? It's our problem," Michelle muttered.

"It's not really our problem either," Nancy smiled. "I'd say that it's more your problem so I think maybe it's good to get other opinions." Nancy watched as her daughter appeared to consider the dilemma she thought she was in but probably no one else would give a second thought.

"Okay," she finally agreed, "but I think you're going to find that they're going to agree with me."

"Well, I won't argue with you, dear. Craig and I are going to the Burger Haven for dinner tonight, why don't you and Connor join us?"

"I'll let you know," Michelle said with a scowl at her mother.

Nancy watched her daughter walk to her bright red Nissan car parked in front of the house. As the sun bounced and sparkled on the shiny surface, it looked liked a layer of diamond dust had been sprinkled across its painted exterior. Michelle shook her shoulder-length blonde hair back over her shoulders and without a glance or a wave at her mother standing in the open doorway, she got into her car. 'Well, that's a first,' Nancy thought sadly.

The problem had begun when she and Michelle had both become engaged within a week of each other. Nancy wondered if that was the problem more than the fact that they were engaged to brothers. 'Could it be that Michelle doesn't feel she's going to get her rightful place in the limelight now that I'm engaged also?' Nancy wondered. The brothers shouldn't be a problem. 'It's not as if I'm cradle snatching,' Nancy thought with a half smile. Connor, Michelle's fiance' was eight years her senior and Craig was ten years older than his brother and three years younger than Nancy. 'Not an embarrassing difference,' Nancy thought since she was just twenty-one years older than her daughter.

"We were lucky that there wasn't a long line-up. Quite often there is because their burgers are so popular. Your mother tells me there seems to be a problem," Craig said as he smiled at Michelle.

"Do you want to explain how you feel, Michelle?" Nancy asked.

"The problem should be self-explanatory. You seem to be the only one who doesn't get it, Mother," Michelle said.

"I don't know what the problem is," both Craig and Connor said in unison.

Michelle turned a withering look on her mother and Craig and took a deep breath. "Don't you think, Craig that it's ludicrous for you and my mother to get married. You and Connor are brothers, for Heaven's sake. We'll be sister-in-laws and you'll be not only my brother-in-law but my step-father too. I haven't heard of anything so preposterous!" Michelle said.

Craig started to laugh but when he saw the look of sheer venom transforming Michelle's face, he became serious. "I'm afraid Michelle that I don't see that there's a problem."

"My mother told you to say that, didn't she?"

"I make my own decisions, Michelle. What is it about your mother and I getting married that really bothers you? I can't help but think that it must be something much deeper than the fact I'm Connor's brother because if it is only about that, there is no one who has a problem with it other than you. Most people who care about your mother and I are very happy for both of us. I'm sorry you can't be happy as well. Your mother and I are both happy for you and Connor."

"I don't think Connor's very happy about the situation either," Michelle said vehemently.

"Do you mind if I speak for myself, Michelle. I don't know what you're so upset about either. I haven't seen Craig this happy for a long time. And if my brother wanted to get picky about it, he had bought the engagement ring for your mother before I bought yours so, based on your attitude, if anyone is going to have to step out, it should be you and me."

"But Connor, this is our first marriage . . ."

"Michelle, I think I know where you're going with this but I think it's time you dropped it right there," Nancy warned her daughter.

"Are you saying that my brother and your mother don't deserve to be happy as much as we do, Michelle because your mother has been married before?" Connor's expression looked as if it had been carved from stone as he stared at Michelle.

"Well, they're . . ."

"Michelle, your mother and I are going to get married with or without your blessing. I know we have Connor's. I think, Michelle, you have a lot of growing up to do and I am saying that as your future step-father. I know you're not going to like me for it but I think someone has to say it."

"I have something further to add to that, Craig. Michelle, I didn't realize before what an utterly selfish and self-centered woman you are. I think maybe we need some time apart to reconsider if we really are meant for each other. I for one, am having some serious doubts about our relationship based on your present attitude."

Nancy felt her heart wrench with sympathy for her daughter but she knew what Craig and Connor were saying were things Michelle needed to hear. Her daughter was headstrong and spoiled and often thought of little else but herself. At least lately that certainly seemed to be the case. Hopefully this experience would make her think about how she treated other people.

Michelle sat, as if momentarily turned to stone, before tears slowly filled her eyes and spilled down her cheeks. Finally, she got unsteadily to her feet. "I think I will go now. I thought as my fiance' you would have stood by how I felt, Connor. But I can see I was wrong. I was wrong about a lot of things, I see now." She began to walk away and then turning, she twisted the ring off her finger. "You'll want this back, Connor."

"Michelle . . . ," Connor stood.

"I don't want to talk to you, Connor. We have nothing further to say."

Nancy started to stand but Craig lay his hand on her arm. "Let her go. I think she's more mad than hurt. And I don't think she got what we were trying to tell her. Let her think about it for a while."

"I don't think she did either," Connor said. "I'm sorry, Nancy. I guess I was a little hard on her but since we became engaged, she's become almost a different person. I don't know what the problem is but she certainly hasn't been the sweet girl I thought I knew."

Nancy could feel the tears well up in her own eyes. She knew both Craig and Connor were right. Her daughter had not behaved well at all. But at the same time, she felt as if she was letting her down by allowing her to leave when she felt everyone was against her. 'But what could I say to her?' she wondered. 'I know Michelle and she won't listen to me, or anyone, when she's in that kind of a mood.'

Craig placed his hand over Nancy's cold one. "I understand how you're feeling, Nancy. And knowing you, I'll bet you want to go after her but I think it would be better to let her cool down first."

"I know you're right, Craig. She'd snap at me if I tried to talk to her now but I do feel guilty."

"You have no reason to, Nancy." Craig looked at his brother's anguished face. "How do you feel, Connor?"

"I do love Michelle, at least I love the girl I thought I knew. But she's been on such a high horse lately and she's become so bossy and critical that now I'm wondering which one is the real Michelle." Connor looked towards Nancy as if hoping for an answer.

"I will admit Michelle can sometimes be self-centered but she can also be a very sweet person. I think now she's excited and I suspect part of it might be that she wanted her wedding to be special and she may think that with Craig and I getting married, it will take some of of the excitement away from her. I can understand that. But we weren't planning on getting married when you were and I'm sure our wedding will be somewhat smaller when we do get married."

"I know that, Nancy. I don't think I handled it well; I jumped all over her when I should have discussed it more calmly. I don't know whether to go after her and try and talk to her or wait until she calms down a little."

"Not that I'm an expert on women, Bro," Craig said as he put his hand on his brother's shoulder, "but I think it would be better to wait. Let her get over being angry so she can think rationally about it and the conversation will go much better, I'm sure." Craig smiled at Nancy. "What do you think?"

"I think you're right," Nancy smiled. "Is that how you're going to handle me?"

"I can't imagine you ever behaving like that. Sorry, I know Michelle is your daughter but I just don't believe you ever would. Okay, let's finish our dinner."

—∿—

"Their wedding was like a fairy tale fantasy," Nancy smiled with tears in her eyes. "It's everything Michelle wanted."

"I'm glad that it worked out for them," Craig said. "They look so happy."

"When are we going to tell them our news?" Nancy asked as they watched the happy couple approach them.

"I think now would be a good time. Michelle's had her moment in the spotlight and hopefully she learned from what happened before or it may be the shortest marriage in history," Craig laughed.

"Congratulations to both of you. You were beautiful, Michelle," Nancy said as she leaned forward to give her daughter a hug. "You make a handsome couple."

"If you've got a couple of minutes, we've got some news," Craig said as he pulled out a chair for Michelle.

"What is it?" Nancy heard the tone in Michelle's voice and groaned inwardly.

"When your mother and I went to Hawaii last month, we got married. We hope you'll be happy for us, Michelle."

Michelle opened her mouth to speak but no words came out.

"I think it's wonderful," Connor said as he gave Nancy a hug. "I know you'll both be happy; you're meant for each other."

"Thank you, Connor. I knew you'd be pleased. Michelle, you haven't said anything yet," Craig said.

"It's done so I don't have a say. I hope you'll be happy," Michelle added reluctantly.

"You never did have a say. This was your mother's and my decision. We'll let you get back to your guests now. I just wanted to remind you that we made every effort to make sure that we didn't take the limelight away from your wedding. We know how important it was to you."

"Thank you. I'm sorry for the way I behaved before."

Nancy glanced at Craig and with a smile she leaned forward to give her daughter a hug. "You'd better join your guests. We'll see you later." As she watched her daughter walk away, Connor turned around and gave them the thumbs up sign.

# HOW NOT TO EAT
# PINEAPPLE

A DRIANNE HAD NOT remembered the rules. That is, until she was lying flat on her back in someone's backyard, her head wedged against the edge of their sidewalk. She, like every other guest at the party, knew the rules. They'd been drummed into her head as a child just as they'd been drummed into the head of every young child. But remembering them in all the frantic excitement of a two year old's birthday party she realized, as she lay in her prone position, was quite another matter.

On the negative side, taking a bigger bite than she could properly chew and talking while she had a foreign object in her mouth was not very ladylike. But on the positive side, she had managed to land on the ground with much grace and as little fanfare as possible. It was true at least, she realized as an afterthought, until she had landed with her head on someone's well-placed foot.

With the piece of pineapple lodged tightly in her oesophagus, she must have remembered other less known rules like, 'don't ruin a good party' and 'don't make a spectacle of yourself' because she had not screamed in agony or writhed on the ground when the pain exploded inside her chest. She distinctly remembered hanging on to the gate with her head down, wondering when the explosion of pain was going to leave her body and vaguely, what she should do about it. She also remembered wondering briefly if they would postpone the party if she suddenly stopped breathing while she was draped over the gate.

As she slowly gained consciousness, she became aware of feeling the cold ground at her back where air had been at her last conscious thought, and with the feel of rough cement against her cheek. She realized belatedly that she had, with no prior planning involved, become the entertainment for this delightful social occasion. However Adrianne, with some embarrassment, knew that her performance wasn't exactly designed for the birthday celebration of a two year old.

Feeling better when she awoke than she'd felt before her debut, she carefully opened her eyes and anxiously tried to sit up. "Wait until the ambulance gets here," a male voice said with the air of authority as he placed his hand firmly on her shoulder.

Lying prone, Adrianne felt conspicuous as many of the party-goers focused their attention upon her. Little faces, their mouths agape in wonder at this aberration on the ground, stared at her. Some giggled, some poked and some jostled her arm, trying to get her attention.

"Why are you lying on the ground?" one small freckle faced little boy, braver than the rest, asked with a sense of determination and a swipe of his runny nose on the back of his grimy hand.

Closing her eyes, in an effort to ignore the circle of people surrounding her, she listened and realized with surprise that a party takes on a much different perspective when you are a guest in a horizontal position.

She decided that it was much like when she was giving birth to what seemed to be a twenty pound baby and the nurses and even the doctor were talking over her perspiring body about the dinner party they'd attended the previous evening. They'd then gone on to talk about their love life, which was the last thing she wanted to think about during that particular experience. In this case, a few chatted about inconsequential subjects as if unconscious of the interruption, one cried while another comforted her sobbing friend as if it was one of them in the prone position. Admittedly, others were trying to console her but all she wanted to do was get up off the hard-packed ground. The small children were eventually pulled away from the upsetting vision of a lady having an unscheduled nap on the newly cut lawn at their special birthday party but not before they had drooled all over her brand new outfit.

After the paramedics left, with assurances from herself that it was unnecessary to go to the hospital by ambulance, she was finally led to a chair to recover from her plummeting blood pressure. As the party resumed, Adrianne had time to think and to reassess her deplorable eating habits. She realized that, as with everything else in life, there are always lessons to be learned.

As the carnival atmosphere subsided, she remembered that the rules were really quite simple. First, 'don't bite off more than you can chew'; rule number two, 'don't talk while your mouth is full' and, rule number three, although a lesser known rule, is, 'don't try to play acrobatics with a pineapple that is in your mouth'. And finally the last rule, when the pain becomes so great that you feel you will burst, say, 'Excuse me please, but I think I'm about to expire'.

Halfheartedly, Adrianne watched the two year old birthday party celebrants frolic around in the back yard playground. As she thought again about the simple rules, she felt there must surely be other, more important ones that should be followed as well. How about, 'cut every morsel of food into minute pieces before placing in your mouth and then chew each mouthful ten times to ensure that nothing is larger than a piece of rice in order to reduce the possibility of it becoming stuck'. This may however, she decided, reduce her dinner invitations if she remained at the table an hour after the last person had departed.

It brought to mind the image of her grandmother nibbling at the corners of her piece of toast and then proceeding to chew each crumb a minimum of twenty times. Adrianne had always assumed that it was her grandmother's worn out old teeth that had encouraged the habit of multiple chews but no, she decided as she mulled the thought over in her mind, her old grandmother knew exactly what she was doing.

Secondly, 'think before speaking, or before answering as the case may be. A simple nod of the head would be quite sufficient. One nod only though or guests might conclude she was a bobble head. And in that case, the two year old toddlers may then consider such a guest to be the hit of the party because of her bobbing head. The scary thought was she could possibly end up in someone's toy box. And if she threw in a smile or two, they might fight over her. The children that is; the adults would think she'd become unhinged from her ordeal—too much pineapple on an empty stomach they'd probably say.

Third, 'don't take deep breaths while eating, only small shallow puffs'. The children would be entranced; they'd all think she was a guppy and want to take her home for their aquarium, she thought. 'Umm,' she mused, 'perhaps this experience could increase my popularity with the toddler population.' Because her popularity, she realized with the adults congregated, was not at an all-time high at the moment.

But probably the most important thing, if she never remembered another rule, was to say, "No thank you, I don't eat pineapple".

# A TRUE APPRECIATION
# OF NATURE

----

D ECIDING TO GET one more camping trip in before the cold weather hit, Fred and Colleen packed up and left their home on the banks of the Fraser River where huge ships, barges and tugs were their daily entertainment.

"Where did you go?" Jasper, Colleen's cynical brother asked.

"To Derby Reach in Fort Langley," they told him as they tried to keep the smiles from their faces.

Jasper shook his head. "You're crazy. Why would you want to camp half an hour away from where you live when you can be more comfortable at home?"

"Well, we can sit beside the river and watch the lights dance on the water," they laughed.

"You LIVE beside the river and you see lights dancing on the river all the time. From your window, no less. You don't even have to go outside to see them."

"And," Colleen logically continued, "we'll be able to sit beside a fire pit in the evening and roast marshmallows and listen to the soft waves lapping onto the shore."

"But you have a fire pit in your own back yard that you can sit beside. I don't understand it," Jasper said with some exasperation.

"Well this way, we can enjoy all that fresh air. It's really quite different, you know," Colleen continued.

"No fresh air at home, eh?"

"Do you know what really makes it different? The fog surrounds us in the morning, wrapping itself around us so we feel like we're in a sheltered cocoon. All the outside sounds are muffled as if we have cotton batting in our ears. We snuggle inside the warmth of the van with moisture streaming down the inside of the windows."

"You think that's fun?" Jasper shook his head again at the idiocy of his sister and brother-in-law.

Ignoring his cranky reply, Colleen continued, "And then when we decide to get up, we make our breakfast in the fog with the sounds of the foghorns on the river beside us. Have you ever done that?"

"Can't imagine why I would want to," he replied sarcastically.

"Where's your sense of adventure, brother dear?"

"Cooking breakfast in a wet, damp fog is not my idea of adventure," he retorted.

"What about the challenge?" Fred asked.

"My golf games are challenge enough. So tell me, what did you get out of your experience?"

"That was the most special part of it all," Colleen told him. "As the fog began to lift, we could see all the beautiful colours of autumn on the trees across the river. And behind us, as the fog dissipated and the sun began to shine through the trees, we were reminded that camping is more than just camping. It is about being out in nature and enjoying what we would otherwise never see had we stayed home. It is about the birth of a new day without being surrounded with all the things that make us prisoners in a world of technology. It is about enjoying what God intended us to enjoy. It is about appreciating those things that cost so little but are worth so much."

Colleen's brother nodded his head thoughtfully. "Maybe next time you go camping, I'll come along with you."

# A SIMPLE QUESTION

WHILE DOING HER will, Carrie's lawyer asked what should have been a very simple question, "Do you wish to be cremated or buried?"

Morbid thoughts! Not liking either idea, she decided to consider her options. As she mulled over the possibilities an idea began to form.

"I could be stuffed," she said as she presented the idea to her five offspring. She knew without words being spoken that none were impressed. "Think of the opportunities. I could attend all of the family functions. You could share me week by week. I can be at every dining room table. I can continue to be part of your lives. You can talk to me. I can't guarantee that I'll answer but I'll certainly be a listening ear. I really can't think of anything nicer!"

They obviously could, she noticed, because not one jumped to say they would take her first. In fact, not one said they would take her, period.

Undaunted with their lack of enthusiasm, she mulled over the possibilities. Hinged knees would be a necessity for mobility. Hinged elbows would also be necessary for family dinners and hinged fingers to hold a wine glass would be a necessity. They must never let her hair go gray and they should make sure her make-up was always applied. She certainly wouldn't want to attend any social function looking like she was more dead than alive. And she definitely wouldn't want to go looking like it was a last minute invitation to attend. But most important, she wouldn't want to miss anything. They know how she hated to miss a good party.

Talking to them individually, each one insisted that while it may be a good idea (although they personally weren't convinced), someone else could keep her. "How could they not want me when they love me?" She began to realize that love her they did but decline her they most certainly planned to do.

She was surprised that cooperation from her offspring was such an uphill battle for her wonderful idea. She decided to try her luck in convincing the grandchildren that a 'stuffed' grandmother would be great to have filling their homes with warmth and love. "I'll always be there for moral support," she enthused. However, she quickly discovered there was no success in that area either. A 'stuffed' grandmother did not seem to appeal to anyone except Carrie.

Not about to give up, she was not convinced she was on the wrong track. Carrie persisted in pointing out the benefits of having a stuffed relative. No one else would have one. And, if nothing else, she would be a conversation piece right up there with ownership of a Sydney Crosby hockey puck. When suggested, Crosby's hockey puck won hands down—after all it was his goal that won.

Carrie began to hear rumblings that she may be stuffed into a closet or a shed instead if she persisted with her idea. It wasn't exactly her idea of being stuffed. With a heavy heart, she began to rethink her idea when her grandson suggested that it might be a good idea after all. She was ecstatic. She finally had a convert. "I'm so happy you like my idea," she said as she gave him a warm hug.

"Yeah," he smiled charmingly in a way only an eight year old can. "I was thinking that if we were to put you out beside the garbage cans, it might help keep the crows away."

Now what was that simple question again?

# A METAMORPHOSIS FROM TOMBOY TO GIRL

A S A GIRL, with a mother who believed a girl should look like a girl, Sarah had a serious problem. There were so many maple branches to swing from, trees to climb, hollow stumps to play in and fern fields for building forts. There were also field mice to catch, creeks to explore, bike rides to take, mountains to climb and chickens to chase.

With her skirt tied between her legs was not how her mother envisioned her only daughter; nor were dresses ripped and hemlines hanging. Her mother's words, 'young ladies don't swing from maple branches or climb trees', fell on deaf ears. Being a 'young lady' was not Sarah's idea of fun.

Her additional dilemma was the fact that she was the only girl in a neighborhood of boys. Her mother tried, with determination and effort, to make a girly-girl out of Sarah but she strongly rebelled against bows, ruffles and lace. How could a girl become a member of a boys' group wearing bows and ruffles? A skirt may be overlooked, as long as she could keep up with the boys, but ruffles would have guaranteed her banishment from this elite group forever.

Although she was the only girl in the gang, Sarah was accepted because she could ride a bike as well and as far as any of them did, could keep up when they hiked and caught as many field mice as the best of them. Admittedly she did have a little trouble trying to put a worm on a hook. The rule was if she wanted to go fishing with them, she had to bait her own line. Shaking slimy creatures that looked as if they had escaped from an alien world onto the ground while trying to stick the hook into them without touching their wiggling bodies was more difficult than Sarah could have imagined and invariably they would fall off into the quick running current of the creek. Losing a worm like that was considered unforgivable, especially when the boys remembered the fact that she had not helped dig the wiggling and squirming creatures from the mud beneath the rocks. After a few lost worms, one of the softer hearted of the boys finally agreed to bait her hook when he saw the hint of tears glistening in her eyes. The catch of Sarah's first little trout was an exciting moment and even the boys were impressed. She wasn't bad for a girl, they all reluctantly agreed.

Sarah felt fortunate to be allowed to be part of this group of boys and knew she was probably privy to more adventures than the average girl has before the hormones of the teenage years change the perspective on what is fun and considered worthwhile to be doing.

However, before that gradual change took place they hung out by the river with its deadly currents and whirlpools, where they were not allowed to go; raided corn fields, which would have given their parents heart attacks had they known; climbed the tower on top of the hill which gave them a heavenly view of the valley below, after having climbed over a barbed-wire fence; and had corn roasts with flames leaping high into the late summer skies. They played in the cold creek in the summer when none of them could swim, skated on the frozen lake in the winters sometimes hearing the ice crack behind them as the weather became warmer; and explored the countryside for miles around from morning until night. They climbed the local mountain following animal trails into the dense bush and trees and investigated deserted miners' shacks and mining equipment. They walked up the logging road, which was forbidden by their parents as well as by the logging company, dodging massive logging trucks as they hurtled down the mountainside weighted down by newly logged trees. They had few rules and fewer that were followed. Sarah had more freedom than she no doubt would have had if she had not been in the company of her brothers and the other boys. Her parents considered she was well protected. While it was true that they looked after her, there was none who looked after them as they pursued one crazy idea after another.

As Sarah grew older and the years passed, cars took the place of bicycles. Sarah and her gang of boys were now able to travel further afield and could drive into the big city exploring unknown territory. During this time she vaguely became aware that a change had begun to take place in how the boys treated her. Most of them, with the exception of her brothers, began not to mind if she had trouble keeping up to them; they patiently waited for her. They gradually stopped expecting her to go on corn raids anymore but she was always invited to the corn roasts and her hook was each and every time baited for her. They stopped swearing in front of her and if someone forgot and did, they were properly chastised by the other members of the group. They began to be quieter and calmer and self-consciously did little favors for her. They began to care what she thought. Sarah was becoming a different entity; she realized she was no longer quite one of them.

Around this time, she was also beginning to realize that it was no longer as much fun to be a tomboy and 'one of the boys' anymore. Her brothers were beginning to openly resent her inclusion in activities with 'their' friends.

It wasn't long after this that Sarah began to be invited on her own, on a 'date'; it was no longer always the whole group and most often her brothers were not included. They were not impressed with this new status quo.

Make-up, curls and shoes with heels suddenly became very attractive; gone was the ponytail, sneakers and her brothers' jeans. She now made an effort to cover her freckles. What had she been thinking, she wondered? She could no longer imagine not wanting to look like a girl. Walking in a lady-like fashion took the place of running, fishing lost its appeal, sitting in a tree was a thing of the past and corn roasts were for kids.

'What happened to her?' Sarah heard her parents whisper.

She spent hours locked in the bathroom standing before the mirror curling her hair, plucking her eyebrows, worrying about zits or just looking at this girl even she hardly knew. It wasn't only her parents who wondered where she had come from.

Her brothers no longer treated her as they had previously done. "What's taking you so long?' they would yell from the other side of the bathroom door. When she'd finally emerge, they'd glare and grumble, "It took you that long to look like this? You wasted your time."

Sarah's brothers and parents no longer seemed to be as pleasant as they once had been; they criticized and complained; their intolerance grew and their patience wore thin. It was a time of disquiet in the household. She couldn't understand how they could all have changed so drastically.

Her hormones had kicked in and her metamorphosis as a girl had begun. Her parents now yearned for their tomboy and her brothers wished for another brother; anyone other than someone who spent so much time in the bathroom.